BLAKEMORT

ALSO BY SHANI STRUTHERS

PSYCHIC SURVEYS PREQUEL:
EVE: A CHRISTMAS GHOST STORY

PSYCHIC SURVEYS BOOK ONE:
THE HAUNTING OF HIGHDOWN HALL

PSYCHIC SURVEYS BOOK TWO:
RISE TO ME

PSYCHIC SURVEYS BOOK THREE:
44 GILMORE STREET

THIS HAUNTED WORLD BOOK ONE:
THE VENETIAN

JESSA*MINE*

A Psychic Surveys
Christmas Novella

BLAKEMORT

SHANI STRUTHERS

STORY
LAND
PRESS

Storyland Press
www.storylandpress.com

ISBN: 978 1 5190 2933 1

For the readers, thank you for joining me on the Psychic Surveys journey.

Acknowledgements

Thanks a million times over to my beta readers, they're my first port of call and let me know whether a story or an idea is actually worth continuing with. For Blakemort, Rob Struthers, Louisa Taylor, Lesley Hughes, Julia Tugwell, Sarah Savery, and Carol Oates (another paranormal author who you should check out, her writing is superb), your input was invaluable. Also, Patrice Brown, thanks for coming up with the title, it's a great name for a (haunted) house. Thanks also to Jeff Gardner, my editor extraordinaire and Gina Dickerson, who's the best cover designer in the land. If you want to get in touch or find out more about my books, contact me on Facebook and Twitter – I'm always on there, spending far too much time – it's a wonder I get any writing done at all!

Foreword

Blakemort, like all my writing, is based on true experiences that have been recorded. For the purpose of this retelling, the house name and location have been changed and the characters fictionalised. Although a stand alone novel it does feed into the main Psychic Surveys series with Blakemort featuring again in Book Six. Enter if you dare, but perhaps leave the door open. You might need a quick escape...

Prologue

THIS is not really a story about me. It's about the house I lived in as a child. A house that couldn't be called a home – that should *never* have been a home. And yet we lived there for years, my family and I. But we weren't the only ones. There were others that resided alongside us. Unseen but lurking; sometimes in dark corners in the dead of night, sometimes in bright daylight, just out of sight, but present nonetheless, watching, waiting. I used to wonder what they waited for. Did they want me to acknowledge them? Shout at the top of my voice that I knew they were there, that I was aware of them? I remember the first time I did. I was alone in my room, a child of seven – nearly eight, in that way that 'nearly' is so important to the young. I was happy; one of the few times I was in that place. The sun was streaming in through the window despite it being mid-winter and I was playing with my dolls – Barbie (of course) and her many friends (most of whom were Barbie dolls too and therefore identical), driving them around in a pink plastic jeep that I considered the very height of chic. They went under the legs of my desk, fixed grins in place, round the perimeter of my wardrobe, whizzing under the bed to emerge the other side, finally stopping outside their tall pink townhouse – part of the Malibu collection. I was engrossed in my game, a bona fide member of the Barbie gang, when I realised the atmosphere had changed. The sun wasn't as bright anymore. The room wasn't as warm. It was cold and growing colder. I started to shiver, pulled the cardigan I was wearing tightly around me. But it was no use. This wasn't the kind of 'cold' that wool could guard against. This could penetrate fabric and skin, burying itself deep into bones and chilling the marrow. It's the kind that lingers in the memory long after it's gone, that once you've experienced it, you can never forget. It's *preternatural*.

I breathed outwards, certain I'd see plumes of mist appearing in front of me. There was nothing but still I began to shake, my teeth chattering in my head, the sound hurting my brain like a woodpecker in the forest gone crazy.

"You're here again aren't you? I can sense you."

At least one of them: the boy.

"I can feel you. I… I've always been able to do that, ever since I can remember. Who are you?"

Swallowing hard I turned my head from side to side, slowly, a fraction at a time, not wanting to frighten them as much as they were frightening me. I had no one to talk to about this ability of mine. I'd tried to talk to Mum once, to tell her what I'd just told the ghosts – that I could sense them. She hadn't been cross with me, on the contrary. 'Corinna, darling, what an imagination you have!" She was laughing and so I had laughed. Perhaps it was my imagination; usually your mum is right about everything. But I knew. Inside I knew. The world has many layers and there's so much that we can't see. That *I* can't see. But once upon a time I could hear…

Corinna…

It was my name being called – no, not called – *whispered*.

Corinna…

As I stood, the dolls in my hands fell to the floor. They'd seemed so alive minutes before, but now they were dead, like whatever else was in the room.

My breathing was ragged and I tried to calm it, but I was a child, a scared and bewildered child. I didn't yet know the techniques involved in maintaining composure when dealing with the paranormal. That house always had an atmosphere. We moved into it when I was five and, apparently, I'd cried solidly for the first week. I was inconsolable, Mum said, but gradually I grew used to the way it was. And there were moments of peace, when whatever was there retreated into the shadows and left us alone, left me alone. But this wasn't one of them. They were the bold ones, not me. Quickly, I closed my eyes and refused to look, my hands rigid by my side. The boy – if that's who it was – was standing in front of me, staring with fathomless eyes. *Ask again what they want.* That's what I should have done. What I *wished* I'd done. Instead, I started screaming, primal fear taking over – fear of the unknown.

The ghost, the spirit, or whatever you want to call it, responded to that scream. Whether from fear or rage I don't know – it could have been both. A thud forced me to open my eyes. The dolls lying at my feet had been snatched up and thrown across the room. *My poor dolls,* I remember thinking. *My poor, poor dolls!* The bed started to shake too, banging from side to side, making an almighty racket that hurt my ears, and the wardrobe door flew open as if a howling wind had got behind it. But none of it could compare to what happened next. I felt pressure around my neck and hot breath on my face. Even now I don't know how that's possible, how a spirit's breath can be *hot*. Spectral hands began to tighten. So easily they lifted me off my feet.

Stop it! Stop it!

I couldn't speak, but I could think.

Please stop it!

And then rather than hear its reply, I saw it scribed in my mind: *I'll never stop. Never. None of us will.*

I was thrown back, hitting the wall as hard as my dolls had.

The door to my room burst open too.

"Corinna, what's all this noise?"

Mum rushed to my side.

"What are you doing down there, sweetheart? And your dolls, one of their head's been split open. Did you do that?" She looked so confused. "*Why* did you do it?"

Not me. Not me.

I wanted so much to speak, to explain, but shock had rendered me mute.

It was them... him. The boy, I'm sure of it, so full of spite.

This is his story really; his, the house's and the other spirits that the house 'owned'. Because it wouldn't let him go, it wouldn't let any of them go. As the boy retreated, still angry with me for screaming, for making such a fuss, and as the sun dared to shine again, albeit tentatively, I suspected something else: it trapped the living too.

Part One
The First Christmas

Chapter One

THERE are many haunted houses in the world. I know that now. But when I was a child I thought I was the only one to experience such horror, so I kept my mouth shut. No child wants to stand out, not for something as weird as that. We took the house because the rent was cheap. It was also grand. I remember my mother saying that: my *single* mother. She'd split from my dad. It was just my older brother, Mum, and I who moved there.

"Wow, kids! What do you think? It's grand isn't it? Much more than we're used to."

She tossed her hair as she spoke – red like mine – and tried to look happy. I say 'tried' because I knew she was sad inside. I was sensitive to emotions too and the divorce between my parents had been hard on her. He'd fallen in love with another woman, or that's what she told us.

When I asked why, she shrugged and said, 'I don't know, it's what people do I guess. They meet someone else and… they fall in love.' There were tears in her eyes but she didn't let them fall. She just kept on smiling, trying to make an effort, to shield us as much as she could. I couldn't understand it though. How could Dad have done such a thing? Mum – Helena – was beautiful with her red hair, her green eyes, and her laughing mouth. She was the most beautiful thing I'd ever seen. We saw Dad regularly after the divorce; he'd take us out every other weekend, usually on the Saturday. My brother was closer to him than I was. He longed for his visits, used to pace up and down the floor, impatient for Dad to arrive. Me? I preferred being with Mum. The 'escape' from Blakemort was nice though; I couldn't deny that, having an entire day's break from it.

I suppose I'd better start describing the house. First of all, it was bigger than an ordinary house, much bigger. It was also very run down, decrepit even – a crumbling mess. The rent was cheap because it belonged to an artist friend of Mum's called Carol, who'd gone to live and work abroad. They'd only recently got back in touch, talking to each other on the phone every now and again and, hearing of Mum's predicament, she'd quickly made the offer. Mum was a graphic designer and worked from home. She earned good money but Dad contributed too, never missing a payment until I, the youngest child, turned eighteen. As Mum said, 'Falling in love with someone else doesn't make you a bad person.' It didn't. But I still hated the fact he'd hurt her. I also hated that we'd moved because of him – to house-sit effectively, to look after a property that didn't *want* to be looked after. But my family was oblivious to that as we approached, they continued walking, straight into its clutches.

Everything was wrong about Blakemort. It was old. Parts of it dated back to the seventeenth century, apparently. Other parts had been added to it over the years, and not sympathetically. It was a higgledy-piggledy house; a hotch-potch – both such amusing terms. But, as I told you, I wasn't amused that day, I was crying.

"Cry baby, cry baby!" Ethan, my brother, sang, his voice cruel rather than melodic.

"Come on, darling," Mum intervened. "It'll be all right."

If only.

Located a few miles from where we'd lived in Ringmer, Sussex – although to me it might as well have been on another planet – in the village of Whitesmith, the house stood very much on its own, as if it wasn't part of the village at all, but was shunned by it. Much of the grounds were overgrown and there were brambles with sharp thorns everywhere. The house we'd lived in previously – the house my parents' had had to sell – was a modern house, semi-detached with light airy rooms. This house was white, but the paint was patchy, peeling off in so many places – a 'dirty' white you could say. It had a large chimney jutting skywards and a silvered oak door studded with wrought iron furnishings, which looked as if it would creak when you opened it. It was off centre too, that's what struck me. The ivy that grew around it not as green as it should be, but withered looking, as if its life force was being leeched. There was no plaque with Blakemort etched on it. Nowhere did I ever see its name written in black and white. It was just what we'd been told it was called. I've often wondered about that, amongst a host of other things. But then again, I suppose it needed no announcement. Such arrogance suited it.

We didn't go in straight away – a subconscious action perhaps on Mum's part, trying to delay the inevitable. Instead, she led us round to the back of the house, down a side path where more brambles and weeds encroached, making the route difficult. Mum did her best to clear the way, stamping with her feet and creating a trail of sorts. Sullenly, I followed in her wake, my thumb jammed in my mouth to stop myself from crying – a tactic that didn't work. If it was unwelcoming from the front, at the back it was forbidding. There was a rounded bay with three windows on the first floor, the frames of which looked rotten. On the ground floor of the bay were two windows and in-between them – again off centre – a glass-panelled door whose splintered surround was painted black. There and then I resolved never to use that door. I had an instinct it led to places as rotten as its frame. There was another set of windows to the right and then a chimneybreast. Further right of the chimneybreast was what I now know to be an add-on: a building that came towards me – the long part of an L. And above, in the roof, were the eaves windows – three of them. Again they seemed to be less than uniformly placed, blackened glass hiding an even blacker interior. Staring at them, I wanted so badly to turn and run, to return to the house that we'd left, to the life that had left us, but all I could do was cry.

"Oh, come on." Mum swept me into her arms. "It could do with some fresh paint I admit, perhaps a few window frames replaced but Carol said it's really quite comfortable inside. And it's big, so big. When it's raining it doesn't matter. There'll be plenty of room for you and Ethan to play. You can even scooter inside!"

None of which consoled me.

"Just leave her, Mum, she's stupid."

"Ethan! That's enough. I've told you before, don't be rude to your sister."

"I wouldn't if she wasn't so stupid."

Back then my brother was always mean to me. When we moved, he was eight to my five and he was surly, even more so than in later teenage years. Of course I now realise that it was mainly due to the separation of our parents. Unlike Mum and me he had dark hair – just like Dad's – and similar features too. We were like clones of our parents, right down to the bickering.

I clung even tighter.

"Don't want to go in there."

"We have to," Mum cajoled.

"No!"

"Come on—"

"Bad place."

"It's not bad, it's just… in need of a bit of love, that's all."

Love? Like it would know what to do with love!

"Bad place," I repeated. "Don't want it!"

"Darling, we have no choice."

Mum's voice was sweet but sadness had crept in; a resignation. Miserable, I started sucking my thumb again. I knew we had no choice.

It began to drizzle so we returned to the front. The removal van was due to arrive soon but we'd brought some stuff in the Volvo Mum used to drive, a few small boxes containing essentials, and she suggested we start ferrying them into the house.

"We can explore too, before they get here. Won't that be fun? A real adventure."

She tried so hard to keep positive.

As we walked, I looked over her shoulder. A part of me said not to, to bury my face instead. I always knew, you see, when a spirit was close by. I'm a 'sensitive'. That's the term for someone like me – who can sense a spirit, but can't always see them. But that day I did see someone, standing in the garden beyond, through the trees and the hedges, most of them winter bare. It was just a fleeting glimpse, one that most people would dismiss, but not me. It was a man, not a child, although, as you know by now, there are children here. He was tall and dressed in dark clothing – as unwelcoming as the house. He had a sneer on his face, I was sure of it, and an expression in his eyes I don't want to think about – even now.

Tears – yet more of them – rolled down my cheeks. As Mum opened the car boot the rain became heavier, as if the weather was mourning alongside me.

The date was December 2nd 1999. December was always a bad month in that house – when most things happened, when the *worst* thing happened. But that would be in years to come. We lived there until 2003. We couldn't stay for 2004. Even Mum agreed with that, no matter how low the rent. Even so, I had years to endure; years that are burnt into my memory. I'm twenty-two now (no 'almost' about it) and I've told this story to no one, not even my closest friends, Ruby, Theo and Ness. They know nothing about Blakemort, let alone my experiences there and how receptive I was during that time. But now... now I have to say something, on paper at least. There's an urge to get it straight in my head – all that happened.

It's fair to say that when you have a psychic ability, de-mons can haunt you. They're attracted to you *because* of that ability and it's hard to persuade them to let go, in some cases nigh on impossible. In many ways, that house is my demon. Although I left it just before I was ten, like so many others, I'm still there. I keep laughing, keep smiling, following the advice of my mother, but it's becoming harder.

That house… that damned house. Will it ever stop haunting me?

Chapter Two

DESPITE Carol having departed only two weeks before, the house had a musty smell to it. Whilst not a stench, it was obtrusive, growing stronger as you climbed upwards. But first, the downstairs – Mum said, 'Let's explore' and so we did.

From the car I'd retrieved a bag of teddies that I usually slept with – three of them in total, each one the equivalent of a comfort blanket. I clutched that bag to my chest, needing all the comfort I could get. Mum inserted the key Carol had sent her into the front door, wiggled it slightly, and pushed it open – rather than a creak, it seemed to groan. Immediately inside was a lobby, meant for muddy boots and hanging coats. Beyond that was the hall, which seemed vast to me, like a cavern, although you must remember that at the time I was small. It was also empty – just a wooden chair placed forlornly in one corner and a side table on which sat an earthenware jug, a few sprigs of crumbling dried lavender placed within it. A chandelier hung from the beamed ceiling – not a twinkly one made from glass, this was blackened iron, hard and unyielding.

The walls were panelled in a dark hardwood and beneath me, the floorboards were dark too, almost black. I took it all in, whilst trying to stop from shaking. Mum was right about one thing: you could scooter in there easily enough.

"Come on, there's a parlour to our left," Mum enthused.

"A parlour, what's that?" asked Ethan.

"A kind of reception room," Mum answered, "where you greet guests."

"Are we going to have guests?"

"I hope so, Ethan. We're a little out in the sticks, but you never know."

There was a pair of heavy green silk curtains at the window in the parlour, which rustled slightly as we entered and another empty sideboard. A painting on the wall of rolling hills caught in the moonlight should have been pleasant but instead it was eerie, and also slightly crooked. Mum noticed too and went to straighten it but when we left the room, I looked back – it was crooked again. To the right of the lobby was a similar sized room – 'the morning room' Mum announced, giggling.

More wooden beams weighed heavily over us in the drawing room but at least it had a decent amount of furniture, including two big squashy sofas, their red material more of a faded pink and an even more washed-out rug lying in-between them. The dining room was also furnished with a long refectory table, gnarled in several places, and six chairs. To the back of the house was the music room. This was the room with the bay windows and *that* door, the one with the black surround.

Ethan started complaining because it had no instruments in it.

"Where are the guitars?"

"Guitars?" Mum answered good-naturedly enough. "It would have had a piano in it, Ethan, not guitars. Maybe we ought to get one, it'd be fun to have singsongs in here wouldn't it, like they did in the old days. Can you imagine…?"

As she said it, her voice trailed off. I noticed she wasn't laughing, giggling, or smiling – she actually seemed uneasy. Could it be that like me she realised the music room was not meant for lingering in, for having a 'singsong'? It was a gathering place certainly, but not for the likes of us.

Almost pushing my brother and me out of there, we entered the kitchen instead – located in the long stem of the L. Not small and cosy, it was large, industrial even, with orange, brown, and cream lino covering the floor in a busy pattern that hurt your eyes. The cupboards consisted of yet more dark wood and the cream worktop had significantly yellowed in places. Looking around, Mum had her 'happy' face back on.

"Isn't it wonderful?" she declared. "Look how many windows there are! On sunny days it'll be a joy to have breakfast in here."

Ethan muttered something vaguely supportive, whilst I clutched my teddies harder. I couldn't forget the music room and how all eyes – no matter that they were unseen – had been trained on me, sensing the one that could sense them. As for the windows in the kitchen, they looked out onto the garden – not a sight I wanted to see again, especially if that man was still present. I imagined him drifting closer on silent feet, peering in through the glass, the look in his eyes intensifying. I yelped.

"What is it, darling, are you all right?"

Before I could answer, my brother pushed past me and almost knocked me off my feet. Mum steadied me then followed after him, calling for me to follow. It was time to venture upstairs. Back in the hall, we started climbing, Mum and Ethan clinging to the bannister. I couldn't because of my teddies, but I didn't want to touch it anyway or think about who'd run their hands up and down it previously.

As I've said, the musty smell was stronger upstairs. Even now, after so many years away, I can smell it. In the lonely reaches of the night when sleep plays hard to get, it drifts towards me, finds its way in, and settles alongside the coldness.

There were five bedrooms in total on the first floor, and my brother darted in and out of each one, wanting to lay claim to the best, although Mum just laughed and told him she was the one entitled to the best. Surprisingly, most of the bedrooms were actually quite small, not grand at all, with beds in only three of them and random items of furniture stored in the other two. Apparently Carol had lived there on her own, as she wasn't married and had no children. Being alone in that house is a thought I find abhorrent – to be the only living person. As we edged towards the room above the music room – the master bedroom – I continued to drag my feet.

Don't want that room! Don't want that room!

I didn't want to go anywhere near it. The atmosphere was heavier on the approach, like wading through treacle.

"This is my room!" Mum declared and I wilted. Sometimes I would wake in the night and when I did, I'd creep in with her and Dad – lately with just her of course – but I wouldn't be able to do that anymore. The floor between rooms was no barrier to what was downstairs – they'd drift upwards easily enough and tower over me whilst I slept; so many of them, far too many. Oh, the tears! They were drowning me.

Mum noticed me loitering in the doorway.

"Come on, come in!"

I stood perfectly still.

"Come on," she said again.

Ethan, who was at the window, turned his head and sneered – I imagined the look on his face to be the same as that of the man in the garden.

I was about to shake my head and tell her no, when I felt a hand at the base of my spine. I tensed, knew to brace myself but it was no use. The hand drew back and then slammed into me with such force that I flew forwards, landing heavily on my knees, the threadbare carpet offering no cushion at all and my bag flying.

"Oh, darling, did you trip?" Mum was beside me in an instant.

"I was pushed!" I wailed.

"Don't be silly, Ethan's nowhere near you."

"Not by Ethan!"

Mum set me on my feet again and gathered my teddies. "Perhaps you tripped over those laces of yours, are they undone?"

She asked the question but didn't bother to check, she just hugged me to her. Behind me, I could hear a faint trace of laughter.

"Let's choose your room!" Mum suggested. It was a mercy to be led away from hers, albeit a small one. "Which one of those that we've seen do you like?"

Ethan had already chosen the one nearest to Mum's but

that was all right, I didn't want it anyway. I think Mum was surprised when I chose the furthest.

"I'm not sure," she said, looking around. It was also small, perhaps the smallest of the five. A frown marred her pretty features, "I think you should be closer to me."

"I want this one!"

"But—"

"Please." There was no mistaking the desperation in my voice.

She looked at me, scrutinised me even. After a moment she bent down so that we were eye-level. Placing her hands on my cheeks, her thumbs drying my tears, she said, "We'll be happy here, I promise. I'll do my level best to ensure that we are."

I didn't know what the word 'ensure' meant then or what 'level best' was but I got the gist regardless – she was saying we'd be okay, that I wasn't to be upset. But she was wrong, so very wrong. And my room, whilst not as bad as hers, was still alive. All the rooms were, as was the house itself.

It lived alongside the dead.

Chapter Three

WE didn't have time to go to the attic as the removal van pulled up, the driver honking the horn to indicate his arrival.

"Never mind," said Mum, "Carol said not to bother anyway, it's only used for storage, it's not habitable or anything. Perhaps we shouldn't go poking around in her belongings anyway. It doesn't seem right somehow."

Remembering how black the eaves windows had appeared from the back of the house, how secretive, I was glad as I was honestly not sure how much more I could bear.

Mum was occupied with directing the men to put what furniture where. Ethan had grabbed his scooter and was getting in everyone's way as they trudged to and fro, Mum shouting at him on several occasions to stop what he was doing and help – not that he did of course. I tried to keep close to Mum but she got irritated with me too and sat me on one of the sofas in the drawing room, telling me in her stern voice to stay put. I drew my legs up and huddled into the corner, doing my utmost not to notice that there was a depression in the cushion to the right of me. Instead I buried my face in my teddies, breathed in their familiar smell, and closed my eyes.

How long I sat like that I don't know but there came a cry from one of the removal men followed by a rush of expletives – or 'bad words' as I used to call them back then. I opened my eyes and listened as Mum's voice added to the mix, asking the man over and over again if he was all right and apologising profusely. I'd been told to stay put but I couldn't. A naturally inquisitive child, I had to go and see what was happening. The man – Mum called him Greg – was lying in a heap at the bottom of the staircase, clutching his ankle.

"Who left that bloody toy on the stair? It wasn't there when I went up!"

It was one of my dolls.

"Oh, dear, oh, dear," Mum was bending down, trying to tend to his ankle, but he wouldn't let her touch it. "It must have fallen out of one of the boxes." She then corrected herself. "I don't see how though, they're all sealed with parcel tape."

"Your kid must have dropped it!"

Mum bristled. "My kid, as you call her, is in the drawing room."

"Your other kid then!"

"It's a doll. My other 'kid' doesn't play with dolls."

"No, he's on the bleedin' scooter, getting in our way!"

Another man appeared on the scene and interrupted. "Come on, Greg, get over it, you've not broken anything. We've got to get on, we've got another job to get to."

The other man helped Greg up whilst Mum stood by, her lips clamped together to prevent her from saying anything more. When they moved away she darted forward and grabbed the doll, holding it in her hands and staring at it, clearly confused as to how it got there. It was Annie – a rag doll, and I'd seen Mum pack her away, stored for the journey right at the bottom of one of those boxes. As I stared I thought I could hear laughter again, an echo of it, but it held no humour, quite the opposite.

I remained standing in the doorway. Mum was distracted so she didn't notice me anyway but I felt safer there, away from that sofa and whoever it was sitting beside me. When everything was in and placed in the right rooms, Mum settled the bill with the removal men. They almost snatched the money out of her hand, hurrying from the house as fast as they could, Greg the only one to look back over his shoulder, his complexion much greyer than when he'd entered the house.

Later that evening, Mum cooked dinner for us and then complained when I wouldn't eat, but only half-heartedly, being too exhausted to insist otherwise. Instead, she cleared the plates and suggested we all get ready for bed, asking me and Ethan if we'd like to sleep in with her – 'a first night treat', she described it. 'All of us together.' Ethan promptly said no and disappeared to his own room and I just started crying again. The thought of being alone in any room in that house was awful but worse still was being in her room, even if she was sleeping right beside me.

Having helped me to wash and change into my pyjamas she took me to my room, not quite believing that I too had refused her. I never had before. I begged her to stay with me until I fell asleep and she agreed – lying beside me and stroking my hair. I think she was humming a tune as well, a Christmas hymn. For some reason it annoyed me, but only vaguely. Like her I was too tired to care that much. Even so, oblivion took a long while to come simply because I was trying to force it, but the next thing I remember was waking with bright sunlight filtering in through the flimsy curtains that fluttered at the window despite none being open. I'd made it to morning! A tiny glimmer of hope began to build as I sat and looked around. The only things in my room were the things that were supposed to be there: my dolls, my dolls' house, my teddies, my clothes, a chest of drawers, a wardrobe, a desk, the bed and me. I was so grateful for that fact I started smiling – a big grin spreading across my face. Of course, being older and wiser, I know that it takes an enormous amount of energy for spirits to do what they'd done the day we moved in – manifest in the garden, push me in the back, make a doll materialise from out of nowhere, whisper and laugh. In-between they'd need to rest, recuperate. That's regarding the spirits. Regarding the house, it was a different beast entirely. It was constant, ever watchful. It watched me as I grinned in relief and so my grin quickly faded. That house – it *despised* us. So vividly that word formed in my mind.

"Mum," I asked a few hours later as we were unpacking stuff from boxes, trying to find a space for everything, with only Mum venturing into the music room to position a vase here or an occasional table there, "what does despise mean?"

She stopped unwrapping what was in her hands – another vase I think – and looked at me with something akin to horror. "Despise? That's a horrible word, where did you learn that?" Before I could answer, her nostrils started flaring and her lips pursed. "It's Ethan isn't it? Honestly, that boy, wait 'til I get hold of him."

She placed the vase back on the floor, stood up, and started shouting his name. Immediately I jumped up and tugged at her skirt.

"It's not him, Mum. I just… know it."

She turned her head sideways to look at me. "How do you just know it?"

I shrugged.

She seemed to consider my words and then knelt again, resumed what she'd been doing. "Like I said, it's a horrible word, mean and nasty."

"But what does it mean?" I asked again, refusing to give up.

"It's… well, it's the opposite of love."

"Hate?"

Mum didn't answer; she just nodded her head.

Having had confirmation, I realised it was no real surprise. I'd gathered as much.

* * *

There are so many incidents similar to those I've described that happened at the house; toys that went missing, only to turn up somewhere else, snippets of voices talking that weren't ours, glimpses of those that hovered near. There was a lot of bad luck too. The vase Mum had placed in the music room was one of her favourites, yet one morning she came down to find it lying on the floor, smashed to pieces. Little things also counted, food got burnt easily, the heating behaved erratically – it was either too high, roasting us, or refusing to come on at all. The hot water would run cold, despite the immersion being switched on hours beforehand. Mum grew more and more frustrated, kept muttering that 'no wonder the rent was cheap, nothing bloody works' but not once did she acknowledge any reason for it other than a mechanical one – and how could I tell her differently? I didn't have the words to explain at that age, and secondly, she'd never have believed me – she didn't *want* to believe.

Yes, there were many things but I can only tell so much. In fact, some things I've forgotten, they only come to mind when I strain to recall. It's amazing how blasé you become, how you adapt. But, of course, there's stuff you can't forget, that's too big to forget, and I'll focus on that. I've already said that the worst times in that house were around Christmas. Such a joyful time of year normally, a time when children grow so excited and we were no exception. That first Christmas, the last of the millennium, only twenty-three days from the day we moved in was one we were looking forward to, despite what had happened to us as a family. Deep down all I wanted was my old life back in the house in Ringmer with Mum and Dad, but I longed for more dolls too, more furniture for my dolls' house, a brand new bike. Ethan wanted a skateboard; he felt he was getting too old for a scooter. He also wanted Dad to join us and asked him to do just that. He didn't but someone else did, another 'inhabitant' that stepped forward from the shadows and picked on me as a conduit.

Chapter Four

BEFORE our first Christmas at Blakemort, I should mention the attic. Like two of the bedrooms, Mum said that Carol used the room on the third floor solely for storage and not to bother going up there, that it was most probably locked. Ethan being Ethan, however, was bored one afternoon and, when Mum was working – she'd set up office in the morning room – he grabbed my hand and dragged me up the stairs.

"Where are we going?" I asked.

"To the attic."

"No, I don't want to!" I protested, happy to take Mum's advice.

"You're such a wuss."

"I am not!"

"You are!"

"No!"

"Then come and explore with me. Don't you ever wonder what's above us when you lie in bed at night? Can't you hear the noises sometimes, like footsteps running up and down, the scratching too, as if something's trapped and wants to get out?"

I ground to a halt on the landing, forcing him to stop. "You can hear those things too?"

My brother's eyes locked onto mine and, for a moment, as we gazed at each other, the four walls that enclosed us fell away. I remember it so well, how hopeful I was, and then he laughed – a sound with as much cruelty in it as the ghost laugh.

"God, you're gullible!"

"Gulli… what?"

"Stupid, you're stupid." When I didn't react he rolled his eyes, grabbed my hand again and continued to drag me. "Just come on," he said.

There's the main staircase in Blakemort and then there's the staircase to the attic. It doesn't carry on from the main one as you'd expect, there's the long, long landing, and then it turns and goes upwards again. Not wide either, it's much narrower. The walls either side of it are covered in a floral wallpaper that has browned with age and is peeling in some corners, as if the house doesn't like such a cheerful pattern and wants it gone. It's strange really because whenever I think of that staircase now, I think of it as hidden, but it wasn't, it was just… tucked away.

Up the second set of stairs, Ethan pushed me in front of him – blocking any attempt to turn and run. *It's okay. It's okay. It's okay.* I repeated those words as I climbed, trying to convince myself. Certainly it didn't feel any worse than downstairs, but even so, I didn't want to go up there. I'd discovered enough about Blakemort.

Close up we could see that the door wasn't locked as Mum had suggested, that it was very slightly ajar. Ethan joined me on the step just outside it, a frown on his face.

"Have you been up here before?" he asked.

I shook my head. "Why?"

"'Cos it's open, that's why."

Open but not welcoming. Nothing about the house was welcoming.

"Go on then," he said, "go inside."

He pushed me again, right into the door and it gaped further. It was so dark in there, as black as the coal we used for shovelling into the fire.

"There must be a light," Ethan said, his hand groping the walls either side of him and finding a pull rather than a switch, which he tugged at.

When it came on, the light was yellow, sickly somehow, failing to illuminate all areas of such a vast space. Plenty of darkness remained. Another smell accompanied the usual musty one, one I couldn't describe at the time but now know to be decay. The room was packed. It couldn't just be with things belonging to Carol, but perhaps Carol's family too, or other owners – items forgotten about or not wanted and left to... rot. There were old chairs, some stacked on top of each other, their mesh frames unravelling, a long refectory table similar to the one in the dining room that we never used, just as gnarled, and a couple of prams, old-fashioned, like no prams I'd ever seen before – used for babies or dolls, I don't know which. A clothes rail too, metal hangers swaying lightly on it, and piles of clothes to the side, as if they'd been torn off. Dark and dreary, I couldn't imagine them being worn again, they were solely the refuge of house spiders. Against the wall, paintings half-covered by a sheet had their backs to us and boxes formed several misshapen towers.

Ethan was agog. "It's full of treasure!"

Never would I have said that, not in a million years.

Walking over to one of the towers, he started prodding. "What's in here do you reckon?"

Why was he asking me? How would I know?

Struggling slightly, he took down the top-most box and placed it in front of him, immediately opening the cardboard flaps and rummaging inside. Whilst he was busy, I took the opportunity to look around – staring at what I couldn't see. I got a sense of children again, some even younger than me, plus adults that cowered, not bold at all. I was amazed. Was it possible that ghosts hide? That they get frightened too?

"Ugh, look!" Ethan pulled what looked like an emaciated fox from the box – my mouth fell open in horror. "How flea bitten is this?"

"Don't touch it!" I yelled. "It might bite you."

"Bite me? How can it bite me? It's dead!" He took the ghastly item and draped it around his shoulders. I can tell you what it is now; it was one of those fur stoles that ladies used to drape across their shoulders, complete with face, legs, and tail – a fashion item of the 1930s. Shocking, absolutely shocking. I honestly think it was at that moment that I decided to become a vegetarian. Funnily enough, of all the things that happened at that house, I find that memory one of the queasiest.

Ethan seemed to revel in my horror but even he appeared slightly disgusted when he finally took it off his shoulders and discarded it to lie forlornly on the floor. He returned his attention to the box. "What else is in here?" he asked again.

I crept closer – curiosity not responsible for such an action, but simply the need to be close to someone living and breathing, even if it was my brother.

He dug further, pulling out smooth oval glass weights but with insects inside them, trapped for eternity. I swallowed – again in horror. There was a rabbit foot hanging from a fob – lucky for some I guess – as well as a framed picture with row after row of butterflies pinned to cardboard, their colours remaining iridescent long after their demise. Rather than appalled, Ethan was fascinated, his dark eyes growing wider and wider. Then his face crumpled. "Oh, I thought there'd be more groovy stuff." He picked up a handful of something. "These are just photos," he said, unimpressed.

The photos joined the fox fur on the floor. Whilst he made sure there wasn't anything else macabre enough in the box to satisfy a little boy's strange desires, I bent down and picked up one of the photos. It was black and white, very old. In fact I wondered if it would crumble to dust in my hands. When it didn't, I examined it carefully. There was a woman dressed in a high-collared black dress sitting upright, her eyes closed, her expression solemn. Two children leant in either side of her, one in a white dress and the other in a frilly white shirt – a boy and a girl, similar ages to Ethan and me. Their eyes were closed too. Why had somebody photographed them sleeping? I picked up another photo – this one of a child much younger, lying on a fur rug, her eyes closed and her hands joined together as if in prayer. Dolls surrounded her, all wearing bonnets and fancy dresses, as far removed from Barbie as you could get. The strange thing about the dolls was they also had their eyes closed. In yet another, two men were sitting, one with his arm around the other – his brother perhaps? He had his eyes open at least but the other man's eyes were closed and he was slumped. Every photo I looked at, the scenario was similar.

They're dead.

As though it had caught fire I dropped the photograph. "What?"

Ethan ignored me. He'd walked over to a rocking chair and was sitting in it, swaying back and forth.

"What did you say?"

That box is full of the dead.

Was it Ethan talking? I couldn't quite make it out. I took a step or two forwards, to peer closer at him. Like the people in the photos, he had his eyes closed.

You're dead too.

I began shaking, violently shaking.

"Ethan!"

Or at least you will be.

"Ethan!"

Soon.

"ETHAN!"

His eyes sprang open; I was so relieved to see it.

"I want to go," I declared, feeling sick to my stomach.

"Go? But we've only just got here, there's lots to see yet."

"We shouldn't be here," I replied. Not meaning just the attic, but the house itself.

There was a wild fluttering above me. I was so surprised to encounter something living aside from us that I screamed and fell back, landing amongst the photos.

Ethan howled with laughter. "You idiot, it's a bat, or an owl. Oh, bloody hell," he said, enjoying immensely that he was out of earshot of Mum and could therefore swear to his heart's content. "How bloody brilliant if it was a bat!"

He scrambled towards me and looked up too but whatever had made the noise was quiet now. His eyes spying one of the glass weights he'd handled before, he picked it up, intending to throw it, to disturb what was there.

"DON'T!" I screamed again, and then more pitifully. "Please don't."

He paused, considered my words, and then mercifully relented. "Come on," he said, "it's hot in here. Besides, I'm bored. *You're* boring. I'm going to play in my bedroom. There's only crap here anyway."

He stepped over me – literally stepped over me – made his way to the door and banged it shut behind him. No longer open, or even ajar, it confined me within – imprisoned me. What was overhead immediately started fluttering again and in dark corners I could sense writhing. Who was it that had whispered? A boy – the same age as Ethan or thereabouts and even worse than him, if such a thing were possible. My arms were on the floor behind me, supporting my weight but I sat up straight and drew them inwards, trying to curl into a ball instead, to make myself tiny, tinier still, invisible. I had to get up, get out of there, but I couldn't move. I swallowed, my eyes darting to the left and to the right. *Who are you? Who's here?*

Something swooped – the bat, the owl, whatever creature it was, black feathers in my face and a smell so bitter it blinded me further. I screamed but worse than that I wet myself, my arms flailing in an attempt to keep the damned thing away. Even in my terror I felt shame that I couldn't control my bladder – that urine was pouring from me – all over the photos, staining them, destroying them. I wanted them destroyed!

"Get away! Get away! Get away!"

Surely my screaming would alert Ethan and he'd come rushing back.

"Get away!"

I pushed myself upwards. If no one would save me, I had to save myself.

The thing that was beating about my head retreated – vanished, as if it had never been. Gone. Just like that. Somehow that was even more frightening – its sudden disappearance. Looking back, I'm not even sure it was real. In fact, right now, at this moment, sitting here writing, I'd bet money it wasn't. It was simply an *illusion*, some kind of magic trick. Certainly, it never appeared again. But alone as I was, or more accurately not alone, I didn't have time to contemplate it. My chest rising and falling, sobs starting to engulf me, snot pouring from my nose, my legs hot and sticky, I could only contemplate escape – but damn my feet, they wouldn't work!

"Mum! Mum! Mum!" I'd call for her instead but if Ethan couldn't hear me from one floor down, Mum wouldn't be able to from the kitchen, or the morning room or the drawing room, or wherever it was she happened to be. I had to change tack.

"He didn't mean it. When he said there's only crap in here, he didn't mean you."

Was that a growl or someone sniggering?

"I don't think you're crap!"

Another noise: definitely a growl.

"I just want to… help."

It was as good a word as any.

"Honestly, that's all I want to do, help."

I was completely defenceless, a little girl against so many. I braced myself, shut my eyes, prepared for something to swoop again or to come racing forwards from the shadows, to launch another attack. Instead, something took my hand – *someone,* with fingers not seen but felt, closing around mine. They didn't pull, or tug, they simply held onto me. I strained to see an outline of the body attached but I couldn't.

That someone cajoled me and got me moving at last, towards the door. They must have opened it because I didn't and yet it swung from its catch. Accompanying me down the narrow stairway, all the way to my bedroom, we passed Ethan's room, the sound of kappowing coming from inside as he forced his soldiers to pit their wits against each other in a seemingly endless battle. It pushed my bedroom door open too. As I've mentioned, I had a desk in my room, just a small one, somewhere where I could sit and draw if I wanted to. But there was a sheet of paper on it now and a pen, not items I'd placed there. Whatever had hold of my hand, it wanted me to write.

Chapter Five

I was five, nearly six, and in terms of writing I could just about manage my own name, Mum, Dad, Cat, Hat, Mat, but very little more. In fact, regarding my own name, a lot of the time I spelt it *Crin* – it was so much easier. I do the same thing now, sign stuff *Crin*, and even encourage people to call me that too. Some do, some don't; Mum steadfastly refuses. What had hold of my hand released it and pulled the chair back, rattling it slightly as though growing impatient.

How I wanted the comfort of my mother but in that moment there was no comfort to be had. Instead, I saw no choice but to do as it wanted. I sat, reached out, picked up the pen, and let my hand hover over the blank sheet.

"I can't," was all I said, trying to explain, but it was no use.

No longer my hand but that of the other, it started gliding over the page, haphazardly at first – I think it was as new to this as I was – making unintelligible marks, lines, zigzags, and circles even. Gradually more control was exercised and marks resembling words began to appear.

"I can't understand," I repeated. What else could I say? But my hand kept writing.

Tears filled my eyes. I wished I could read better, that I could understand what was going on.

"Who are you?" I asked. He or she – I didn't even know that much – seemed gentler than the others I'd encountered, less vicious. I even wondered if we might be friends. Ah, I was such an innocent! The being couldn't answer me, not in a way I'd understand, only through writing – a way that made no sense to me at all.

Frustration rose. "Talk to me instead!"

Normally a shy child, reserved, I was sometimes prone to the odd tantrum. I broke the hold it had over me, stood up, and threw the pen down. I didn't want to write anymore, what was the use of it? Growing angrier still, I leant forward with the intention of picking up the paper and of tearing it to shreds, and that's when this benign being became less so. It shoved me hard, sending me flying back to land at the side of my bed. In an equally fighting mood I scrambled to my feet and dived forwards again, determined to destroy what it had created. But I couldn't move! It was as if a wall had sprung up in front of me. I brought my fists up and beat at the air, yelling still.

What a sight I must have looked, my hair wild, my clothes awry and stinking of urine! Just as I sometimes did with Ethan I continued to retaliate, remembering that memorable time I'd shut his fingers in the doorjamb. He'd been taunting me about something, calling me names again – stupid, dumb, idiot – the usual. It was in my bedroom in our old house, just before we moved. When he turned to leave, he trailed his fingers along the width of the door, into the hollow – I noticed, seized my chance, kicked out and slammed it shut, his hand in the wrong place at the wrong time. The cry he emitted was so satisfying… for about a minute. And then it burst open, Mum standing on the other side – a look of abject horror on her face.

"What's happened? What the hell's happened? Oh, Ethan, are you okay, darling? What did you do?"

"SHE did it!" Ethan continued to scream, pointing at me. "She slammed the door on my hand deliberately!"

"Corinna?" Mum looked as if she didn't believe a word – not her small daughter, surely? She wasn't capable. But children are far more capable than they look.

Ethan was making such a song and dance about it, clutching his hand to his chest, and shouting the house down. There was even a spot of blood, staining the carpet beneath his feet, the crimson a stark contrast to the oatmeal. I stood there, hoping Mum wouldn't believe such a thing of me. But my silence was damning.

"Corinna, was it you?" she said whilst hugging her other injured child to her.

Should I lie – say no?

"Corinna?"

It was bad to lie wasn't it?

"CORINNA!"

"Yes," I blurted out. I couldn't lie. I shouldn't.

If only I had.

I was confined to my room for the rest of the day – a beautiful day, full of sunshine, we'd been promised a trip to the beach but that was cancelled, as I had to learn that 'violence will not be tolerated in this house.' But violence was tolerated at Blakemort, all the time. Because no one believed it was being administered.

The wall – for want of a better description – forced me

all the way onto the bed, lowering itself, coming closer, closer still. I held my hands out to fend it off but they were forced back too. It was bearing down, the feeling similar to being buried alive, or at least how I imagine that to be, as suffocating. Panic flooded through me; fear too, wiping away any boldness that might have surfaced, obliterating it entirely. I couldn't breathe. I was going to be crushed. Surely I was going to be crushed!

I won't tear the paper up. I won't.

Still the weight was on me.

Promise. I promise.

Was this it? Was I going to die? Upstairs, in the attic, that's what I'd been told was going to happen, but so soon?

Please listen to me!

I *was* going to die. This thing was going to kill me. My chest seemed to cave as air was forced from my lungs. Everything was going black, my sight failing too.

"Ethan, Corinna, come down and see who's here!"

I heard the words but they were so far away.

"Come on, we have a visitor!"

We had a visitor? Well, I had a visitor too – an unwelcome one.

"Ethan! There you are. What have you done to your hair? It's all over the place. Get it combed. Where's your sister? Fine then, if you won't tell me, I'll go and find her myself. She must be in her bedroom. Oh, this is so exciting!"

Just before consciousness deserted me, Mum burst into the room.

She took one look at me and hurried over.

"Darling, this is no time for a nap. Come on, Aunt Julia's here!"

* * *

"Ethan! Corinna! Come and give me the biggest hug."

Aunt Julia was different to Mum, even though they were sisters. Mum, whilst not petite was of medium stature, but Julia was tall. Amazonian I think you'd call it, with blonde hair that was straight rather than red and wavy. She had a sprinkling of freckles on her nose but no more than that and this wonderful warmth to her that I always responded to. Running, I leapt into her arms. If she noticed that I smelt peculiar, that I was damp, she didn't say, didn't even so much as wrinkle her nose, she just hugged me close, and to this day, I'm grateful that she did. That she realised how much I needed hugging in that moment. What had happened, the battle that had been fought upstairs, it was over – for now. But I hadn't won it. Oh, no. That piece of paper – I wouldn't tear it up, I'd keep it. I *had* to keep it.

"Oh, sweetheart, how lovely to see you."

With one hand Aunt Julia was stroking my hair. Ethan hovered close by, clearly waiting his turn but I didn't care, he could wait. He'd left me in the attic, had shut me in and I hated him for it – *despised* him.

Finally, I was released and Ethan saw his chance, stepped forward, and elbowed me aside. I might be making this up in retrospect but I think my lip curled and I snarled at him, actually snarled. But like I say, I could be making that up. I'm sure if Mum had caught me snarling, she'd have smacked my legs. Talking of which, Mum finally noticed there was an odour.

"Darling, have you… you know…?"

Shame returned with a vengeance.

"I… I…" But how could I explain? How could I possibly explain?

Mum's face fell. "Oh, dear," she said, reaching for my hand, but I didn't reach back. I didn't want anyone to hold my hand again.

"Come on," she prompted, wrinkling her nose.

Aunt Julia looked over Ethan's shoulder. "What's the matter, Hel?"

Mum gestured towards me. "She needs a bit of a wash."

"A wash?" Aunt Julia turned towards me too, my face burning as she did. There was laughter again, coming from the direction of the music room – no one to hear it but me. She let Ethan go. "I'll take her upstairs if you like, run a bath and whilst I'm at it, she can show me around." Focusing on me, she added, "Would you like that, sweetie? You and me together exploring this big old house?"

As much as I relished time alone with Aunt Julia, no I didn't want to go exploring. I wanted to run, as fast and as far away as I possibly could.

Pushing Ethan gently away from her, ignoring his disgruntled look, she held out her hand. I was happy to take hers at least. As I did, the laughter died down.

Aunt Julia was Mum's younger sister and the reason they looked so different was because they had different dads – neither of them took after their mother, my Nan, who had died when I was a toddler. I sometimes wonder if the fact she came from a broken home meant Mum accepted the break-up of her own family so readily. But what do I know? Nothing really on that score, because Mum never talked about it, not then and not now. She just… accepted it. Still, I couldn't help but wish she'd tried harder with Dad. If she had, we wouldn't have had to leave our house. We wouldn't have ended up at Blakemort – all that had happened would simply *cease* to have happened. That's what I thought anyway. Now I wince. Why do we always think it's the woman who should try harder? Why not the man? They get away with so much.

Aunt Julia wasn't married and neither did she have kids. That's why she loved us so much, I think. She doted on Ethan and me, if I'm truthful me especially. Stepping aside, she let me lead the way and so I did, again seeing no option but to carry out the wishes of others. Mum asked Ethan to come and help her in the kitchen, but he was disgruntled about that too – reckoned he'd drawn the short straw. If only he knew.

I didn't want to climb those stairs again and face what was there. But was downstairs any better? Earlier, when Mum had dashed into my room, whatever was holding me down had disappeared as quickly as that which had swooped in the attic – another magic trick. I was able to sit up again and breathe, although not hide the shock and bewilderment on my face. Little matter, as Mum didn't notice anyway.

I showed my aunt around, hesitating at Mum's bedroom again but she went in anyway, declared it 'nice', nothing more, nothing less, left it, and headed for the bathroom instead. The bathroom was a cold room – even submerged in hot water you'd shiver. Whenever I had to use it, I tried to do so as quickly as possible, never lingering. Aunt Julia ran the taps and I half expected dark matter to gush out but it was only ever water – albeit water that had a slight tinge to it. 'It's because of the piping,' Mum had already explained to me. 'It must be as ancient as Blakemort itself', but somehow I never bought that. Despite scrubbing at myself with soap and a flannel, it was impossible to feel clean in that house.

After I'd been bathed and wrapped in a towel, and with Mum and Ethan still busy downstairs preparing dinner, we walked to my room.

"I'm dying to see it," Aunt Julia declared, her choice of words not the greatest under the circumstances.

On entering, she said it was 'lovely' but it was just a room with cream walls, the paint patchy in places and fluttering curtains at the window. It was far from lovely.

"Let's get you some clean clothes," she continued, walking over to the wardrobe.

In the centre of the room I stood still, steadfastly refusing to look at the piece of paper on my desk, to acknowledge it. There remained a trace of boldness in me despite what had happened. But it began fluttering too, capturing the attention of my aunt. Instead of opening the wardrobe doors, she turned her head towards the desk.

"What's this?" she said, beginning to change direction.

"No, don't…" I began, but too late.

She had reached the desk, picked up the piece of paper, and read the words I wasn't able to. Her eyes widening as she managed to decipher the scrawls, she grew stormy when usually she reminds me of a bright summer's day.

"Corinna?" she questioned, waving it in front of me.

I did what I always did in awkward situations at that age – I burst out crying.

Immediately she was all concern.

"Oh, it's okay, it's all right, sweetie," she said, clutching the piece of paper but hurrying over to me. "I know it's not you that's responsible. You can't write yet, surely." Her lips pursed, much the same way as Mum's did. "And even if you could, you wouldn't write this." She paused again and tried to make sense of it. "It must be Ethan," she declared. "That flaming Ethan! This is taking teasing to a whole new level."

Abruptly releasing me, she marched out of my room and back downstairs. That was the day before Christmas Eve. On Christmas Day, she left.

Chapter Six

ON the way down, I tried to tell Aunt Julia it wasn't Ethan responsible. As angry as I was with him it wasn't fair that he should be blamed for something he didn't do. She wasn't listening. Perhaps that was just as well. After all, who was I going to say did it – a ghost? I could imagine the look on her face if I did.

With me behind her, now running to keep up, she barged into the kitchen, waving the offending piece of paper in front of her. Mum, who was stirring something, or rather had her hand over Ethan's hand, making him stir it, looked sideways at us.

"What's the matter, Ju–?"

She didn't get much further as Aunt Julia erupted.

"This! This is what's the matter, Helena. She's a five-year-old girl for God's sake. What the hell is Ethan doing writing this sort of stuff and leaving it in her room? I don't even care if she can't read it yet, it's not right. It's… weird."

"Ethan?" Still Mum was thunderstruck.

"Yes, Ethan!"

Before I could interrupt to try and save Ethan again, Aunt Julia slammed the sheet of paper onto the yellowed worktop and said, "Take a look, go on… see for yourself why I'm so upset."

Wiping her hands on her apron, Mum did as she was asked, her expression growing even more bewildered as her eyes scanned what was laid out beneath her.

"What? I don't understand. Ethan?" She shook her head as if to try and shake from memory what she'd seen. "Why'd you write this?"

"Write what?"

"THIS!"

Mum shouting made both my brother and me jump.

"I didn't write anything!" he yelled back.

"Don't lie."

"I'm not."

"He didn't!" My voice was small compared to theirs and easily lost.

"This is…" Mum screwed up her nose. "Horrible!"

"I've done nothing wrong," Ethan continued to protest. And then, still indignant, he pushed past Mum and started to read aloud. "House, Dead, Hate, Hurt, Kill, You, You, You."

As Mum said, horrible words – a horrible sentiment – but there was a strange relief in hearing them at last.

"I know they argue, Hel, but honestly, this is beyond the pale."

Tears were springing to Ethan's eyes. "I didn't write it!"

"Of course you did!" Aunt Julia responded.

"Hang on," Mum turned on her sister. "Ethan's my child, let me deal with him."

But Aunt Julia was just as fiery as Mum. "I think you'd

better, Helena, this is bullying of the worst kind. I can't think why you haven't nipped it in the bud before."

"Don't tell me how to bring up my children."

"I'm trying to help."

"Coming in here and shouting the odds. You think that's helping?"

Mum squared up to Aunt Julia, the two of them standing face to face, the difference between them even more pertinent – Aunt Julia, a warrior woman, Mum, a red dragon and capable of breathing fire.

"He's my son, Ju, and if he wrote those words, I'll deal with him, not you."

Ethan was crying in earnest now and I have to say, I couldn't blame him.

"I just want to help," Aunt Julia insisted. "Things have obviously got a bit much for you lately."

"I'm on top of my game, thanks."

"It's hard being a single parent, I get that—"

"I don't need telling."

"Then let me help."

"YOU'RE NOT HELPING!"

Mum's voice seemed to cause a mini-earthquake as pots and pans began to rattle, and the drawers too. The smell of burning filled the air, and that's what finally distracted Mum. "Oh, God, the chilli!"

No longer in a fighting stance, she rushed over to it, but it was ruined apparently, sticking to the pan. "But I turned the flame down," she was muttering. "Didn't I?"

The kitchen implements stilled. No one seemed to have noticed what had happened to them but me, but then Mum and Aunt Julia were focused only on each other, and Ethan, he'd been staring at them in terrified awe. Once again, the spirits had played to the gallery – the gallery with only me standing in it. Mum was furious.

"Look what you've done with your wild accusations, you've ruined dinner."

"I wasn't the one who left the heat up high."

"Nor did I!" Mum screeched before once again turning to Ethan. "Did you turn the flame up? It was you, wasn't it? Who else could it be?" She was accusing him as readily as Aunt Julia had. Poor Ethan. Hot tears seemed to sizzle on his cheeks as he ran from the room. I had to dart out of his way or he'd have mowed me down. He ran up the stairs crying over his shoulder as he went. "I hate you, I hate all of you."

That house, so easily it inspired that emotion.

Mum kept blinking her eyelids, trying not to cry. Even Aunt Julia looked shocked. "I'm sorry, Hel, I shouldn't have come in here shouting the odds as you say. I should have talked to you privately."

"Damn right you should," Mum mumbled, doing her best to resurrect dinner.

"It's just… Look at that paper, look at it. Those words seem *carved* onto it. If it was Ethan, and I don't know who else it could be, he's really troubled. You know, what with the divorce and everything…"

"Don't you think we all are?" Tears fell from Mum's eyes now, a torrent of them, like a dam bursting. "Like you said, it's hard, Ju, bloody hard!"

"Oh, I know, I know." Aunt Julia bridged the gap between them and tried to hug her. At first Mum was having none of it.

"You don't know. How can you? You've no bloody idea."

"Hel, come on."

"No!"

But Aunt Julia was bigger than Mum and more determined. Against her wishes, Mum was enveloped in her sister's arms and, after a moment, she stopped resisting, needing that hug as much as I had earlier.

I looked on, hoping that was it. That we could just get on and prepare for Christmas. That someone would take that sheet of paper and destroy it. No one did.

* * *

Christmas Eve is almost as good as Christmas Day isn't it? I think it's the anticipation, there's so much to look forward to, so much to hope for. After the argument, we ate burnt chilli with soggy rice and then we went to bed, all of us exhausted. Aunt Julia was staying in my room on a mattress on the floor. It was her idea, but after what had happened I was so pleased she was beside me. She'd sort of made up with Ethan, apologised to him, told him to speak to her if he had any 'issues' but Ethan had that look in his eyes – that 'unforgiving' look. It didn't seem to worry Aunt Julia but it did me. I tried to speak to him too, to tell him I'd never said it was him who wrote on that paper, but he just brushed me off, too lost in his own fury. As for that paper, at breakfast the next morning – on the hotly anticipated Christmas Eve – it was gone. When Mum temporarily left the kitchen, I opened some drawers, searching for it, and sure enough it had been stuffed into one of them, shoved down the side – out of sight, out of mind, but not my mind. I couldn't forget it.

Mum came bustling back in, Aunt Julia and Ethan trailing in separately behind her. For breakfast she whipped up scrambled eggs and we crowded round the table to eat it. At first the atmosphere was sullen but gradually it lifted and Aunt Julia, determined to atone for yesterday, offered to take us shopping. She wasn't flashy, Aunt Julia, but she was stylish with close fitting clothes, and perfect hair and make-up. Mum, on the other hand, liked loose skirts and blouses, just a hint of lipstick and lots of bangles on her arms. It's a look I loved, reminding me of something exotic, a gypsy woman, and one I adopted when I grew older, although I added a bit of an Emo twist. I think with our Titian curls, we dress to suit our hair! But I digress. As I said Aunt Julia wasn't flashy, but she had a good job in finance, and a flat in London, she could afford to spoil us a bit. In some ways she was everything Mum wasn't, but I'd never seen resentment between them, never witnessed an argument before – only ever in that house.

And there was more to come.

Chapter Seven

LEAVING Blakemort, we all piled into Mum's Volvo and headed into Brighton. First on the list was a visit to Santa, who was holding court in the shopping mall. Ethan refused to go in but I was beside myself, the wait in the queue nothing less than excruciating. I almost wet myself again, but this time with pure excitement. I must add here that Ethan and I knew most of our Christmas presents came from Mum and Dad, they encouraged us to believe in the magic of Santa but not that he spent a fortune on every child! Rather it was visiting him in his grotto that was of the utmost importance, the sheer thrill of it. Not that Ethan thought so, hence his refusal. It was so different to how he was last year, when he'd been as eager as me, if not more so.

Afterwards, we headed to Browns Restaurant for a burger and a milkshake – another treat. It was there that I opened the gift Santa had given me – Mum had told me to wait until we were sitting down, to savour the moment, rather than rip into it. As the waitress brought our drinks over, I retrieved the gift from her handbag, my fingers trembling as I peeled back layers of cheerful wrapping paper, resplendent with reindeers and striped candy canes. What I saw caused me to tremble for different reasons. It was a notepad and pen, an innocent enough gift; some might even say a welcome one, but not me, not after what had happened. Everyone around the table stared at it for a few seconds before I threw it from me.

"Don't want it!" I declared.

Mum didn't react initially. She continued to stare and then she placed her glass down and picked it up instead. "It's just a notepad and pen," she mumbled before tucking it into her bag, out of sight, out of mind again.

The gift soured lunch. Even far from it, the house was having an effect. We did a bit more shopping afterwards, waited for night to fall so we could admire the lights the Council had strung up in the city centre, which weren't that impressive to be honest, and then we trundled home to have cheese and biscuits for dinner – something of a family tradition on Christmas Eve. I think I shook all the way back to Blakemort, Mum taking it easy on that long dark country road that led to the house, the trees towering over us to form a tunnel. Even in daylight the sun had a hard time trying to filter through. As we travelled, I glanced at Ethan. He was biting his nails, a dreadful habit of his, right down to the quick.

Pulling into the gravel driveway, a crunch beneath our feet as we exited the car, the house reminded me of a spider, waiting to strike. It's strange with Blakemort. It didn't want you there but it didn't want you gone either – it fed on you.

Keeping my eyes on the ground, we walked to the front door, all of us taking our time, no one in a rush to get inside. Mum was going to light a fire in the drawing room, where we'd erected a Christmas tree a few days before, and had already stacked up logs beside the coal bucket. They were neat no more. As we entered that room, single file, Mum groaned. "Who the hell did that?"

The logs were scattered everywhere, some of them charred, as if they'd been burnt already.

"What a mess. What a bloody mess!"

I don't think I've ever heard Mum swear so much as when she was in that house.

"They probably just took a tumble," Aunt Julia replied. "Let's get it cleared up and the fire sorted. It's freezing in here."

Which was strange as it was a mild December and certainly not freezing outside.

"Brrr," Aunt Julia made a show of hugging herself. "Doesn't your heating work?"

"It does, when it wants to," answered Mum irritably. "Which is hardly ever."

I looked at the Christmas tree, half expecting to see it dashed to the floor too, but it was intact. Incredible really come to think about it, as it was such an obvious target. But that tree, once adorned, was never felled, not in all the years I lived there. The ghosts, the spirits, the entities, they were more original than that.

Mum and Aunt Julia coaxed the fire into life whilst we went upstairs to change into our pyjamas. Mum never put the presents under the tree until late on Christmas Eve; she knew we'd never be able to leave them alone otherwise, continually prodding and poking at them. Usually, she hid them in her bedroom. They were certainly safe there, from me anyway, but Ethan wanted to go in.

"Come on, they'll be under her bed or in the wardrobe or something."

"No. Mum will get cross."

"Mum knows we go in and look, we always do."

"No," I said again.

Ethan screwed up his face. "What's wrong with you, you used to be fun."

"I don't like Mum's room."

'Why not? It's fine.'

"It's not."

For a moment Ethan was quiet and then he moved forwards and grabbed my arm. "What's wrong with it, tell me." And then slightly more agitated, "What's wrong with this house, Corinna?"

So he knew, like me he knew.

"It's—"

There was a huge crash, coming from the direction of one of the spare rooms – the one next to mine.

Ethan's eyes widened. "What was that?"

Before I could answer Mum called up the stairs, asking the same question. Hearing no response, she started climbing, Aunt Julia behind her.

"It wasn't me," Ethan said, when she reached the landing. "It came from in there."

The door to that particular room was shut and had been since the day we'd arrived, only briefly had we all taken a look in there. It was one of the storage rooms.

"Oh, for goodness' sake." Mum was still irritable. "I never said it was you, did I?"

Without hesitation she opened the door. I stood rigid, expecting a figure of some sort to come rushing at us. It's funny isn't it, how a figure as familiar as a human being can be so damned terrifying. No such thing happened, but there was another mess to be cleaned up. A mirror – large with an ornate surround, French apparently and an antique – had crashed to the ground and glass lay in smithereens.

"I don't bloody believe it," Mum declared. "I just don't."

"Point me in the direction of the dust pan and brush and I'll do it later," said Aunt Julia. "Right now, we need to eat, the kids must be starving."

We were. The burger we'd consumed had been hours ago.

Without changing our clothes, we all went down to the living room, the fire was roaring but not lending much warmth. It was still cold. Mum cursed again then left us and went into the kitchen. When she returned her face was like thunder.

"What's wrong?" asked Aunt Julia.

"It's the cheese," she replied. "I only bought it yesterday, but already it's gone mouldy. And before you say it, no I'm not talking about the blue, I'm talking about the cheddar, the Brie, the manchego, everything. It's all sodding gone off!"

* * *

Ethan got his skateboard and I got my bike. Dad had also sent lavish presents. '… trying to make up for his absence,' I heard Mum say to Julia, '… for the damage that he's done.' We must have thought so too, because somehow his gifts seemed to elicit no joy, only sadness, no matter how shiny and new they were.

After all the gifts had been opened, Mum and Aunt Julia went off to prepare Christmas lunch – roast turkey with all the trimmings. Ethan and I remained in the living room, but not for long.

"Bring your bike and let's go to the music room," Ethan suggested. "It's a great place to skateboard."

My heart sank but how long could I keep saying no to him? Besides it'd be all right, wouldn't it? Everything's all right at Christmas.

As I followed him towards it, I was sure I could hear whispering, but it was very faint. Ethan was right, the music room was perfect for hammering up and down, the expanse of floor space too tantalising to ignore. We could have gone outside I suppose but it was raining again – which was such a disappointment as we'd prayed so hard for snow – and neither one of us fancied getting wet. Ethan started practicing immediately and I did too, not hard really as my bike had stabilisers.

"Take them off," Ethan called over his shoulders. "Practice properly."

I ignored him and continued to peddle.

There was laughter from the kitchen – good laughter – the sound of Mum and Aunt Julia getting on again. I smiled to hear it.

"Take the stabilisers off," Ethan called again.

I rolled my eyes at him.

"Go on, don't be such a chicken."

"I'm not a chicken," I protested at last.

"You are, you're a chicken," he retaliated, but it wasn't with his usual venom, he sounded cheerful. "Chicken,

chicken, chicken."

"I'm not," I said again, but cheerful too. The day wasn't turning out so bad.

I gripped the handles harder, peddling fast, really getting the hang of my lovely new bike with its pink and white frame and white leather handles. Mum had spared no expense; this was the bike I'd set my heart on. Peddling faster, faster still, I was on my fourth or fifth run, approaching the door that led into the garden. I had to brake, or I'd be in danger of going through it. I wasn't overly panicked though; there was still some distance left. Beside me, Ethan was keeping apace. My hands closed around the brakes and I squeezed. Nothing happened. Frowning, I squeezed again... and again. Why weren't they working? They'd been just fine before. Even so, I continued hurtling forwards. We were both going to go through the door! I took my feet off the pedals – that would work surely? But they continued spinning.

"Mum! Mum!" I yelled, panic setting in, unlike Ethan, who was laughing, enjoying the thrill.

"MUM!"

"Chicken, chicken, chicken!" Ethan was at it again.

The glass door – the one I hated so much, loomed closer, ever closer. I had a sudden vision, of my face cracked and bleeding, shards of glass sticking out like some hideous mountain range. And my eyes! Oh, my eyes. They'd been ripped to shreds. The vision caused me to scream, startling myself but also Ethan, who lurched towards me, knocking me off my bike just a fraction or so before we reached the door. It sent me flying into the wall instead, only my bike continuing onwards, bang smack into the frail pane and shattering it completely.

"Oh, good God! What now?"

It was Mum, at the entrance to the music room, wild-eyed, Aunt Julia the same.

A blast of air enveloped me, icy in its embrace. Ethan, who was on top of me, pushed himself off, one fist striking out as he did, cursing me for having screamed, for toppling us both.

"Don't you dare hit her!" It was my champion, Aunt Julia. She grabbed him and hauled him to his feet. "Don't you bloody dare, you brat!"

"JULIA!" Mum yelled.

Aunt Julia whirled towards her. "You've lost control, Helena, completely."

I was wailing, Ethan was wailing. The ghosts, they started laughing again.

Mum snatched Ethan to her whilst Aunt Julia knelt down to see to me.

"Is she okay?" Mum asked, her voice as brittle as the glass.

"She's fine," Aunt Julia muttered. 'No cuts or bruises that I can see."

"Good. But I'm afraid I can't have you staying here any longer, Julia, I'd like you to pack your bags and leave. Children, go into the kitchen now. Dinner's almost ready."

Part Two
The Second and Third Christmas

Chapter Eight

OUR first Christmas was over and it had been a disaster. Aunt Julia did as Mum asked and readied herself to leave, giving only me a kiss goodbye. I was inconsolable but Mum was not in a soothing mood. Instead she tried to patch the broken pane with cardboard and whilst she did dinner was ruined. None of us had an appetite anyway.

We didn't want to play any more with our bike or skateboard either – like the presents Dad had got us, they'd lost their shine.

On the twenty-seventh we went to Dad's and then, a few days later, it was the New Year celebrations, Mum allowing us to stay up and count down the minutes on the TV as one century yielded to another. A momentous occasion – screams and cheers poured into the room courtesy of that tiny box. Yet to me, it seemed anything but. Rather, I clung to what was gone and could see nothing to look forward to. Time was a strange thing in that house. It passed, as it always did, but slowly, so very slowly. It only ever went fast when we were outside the house, at school perhaps, or out shopping, or with Dad on a Saturday. Then it seemed to be on a spool, winding us swiftly back towards it, whereupon it would move at a grudging pace again.

The days, the weeks and the months passed. Lots more happened, but as I've said, for the purpose of this retelling I want to focus on the main events – principally Christmas. Even so, throughout the year things went wrong. The pane in the music room door had to be replaced, costing Mum money she could ill afford. The heating continued to play up, either not coming on at all or going into overdrive. One time I touched the radiator, even though I'd been told not to and it burnt my hand. I couldn't believe it; it was like touching flames leaving a sore red patch that took its time to heal. Light bulbs overhead kept fizzing and popping. Mum said they cost a small fortune to replace. The milkman used to leave two pints a day but too often the milk was sour, so Mum finally cancelled the order. Strangely enough though, the milk she bought from the supermarket soured just as easily – she never could work it out. But I could. Nothing could thrive in that house – food, plants, even us. As a family we failed to thrive and Mum lost work. She was good at what she did, previously in demand but clients got fed up with her failing to call them back. "But I never got your message," she'd protest. "Are you sure you left one?" Of course they had, but nothing was ever recorded, the answer machine wiped clean as soon as the last sentence was uttered. With less money coming in, we couldn't buy as much food and I swear we began to look ill, the three of us – our pallor grey. I'd been quite plump before we moved to that house, a good covering of puppy fat on my bones, but by the time we left my ribs jutted out. As I said, the hauntings continued, the scraping noises above in the attic where I hadn't dared venture again, the low, cruel, laughter, the sensation of being followed wherever I went, the eyes that were always on me. And the flies. I haven't yet mentioned the flies. They were incessant. No matter what Mum did, what sprays and repellents she bought, or how many times she swatted at them, there were always flies in that house – swarming over everything. The writing too, that wasn't a one-off incident. Whoever had guided me had more to say.

Having turned six, it was imperative I learnt to read as soon as possible so I could understand what was being scribed. We think the young don't know much. We assume their common sense is fairly limited, but when I reflect, I was mature beyond my years. What was happening forced me to grow up fast. I had a sense that if I learned what was being said, it would empower me in some way. Mum couldn't believe how eager I was to have extra-curricular lessons with her – she was stunned in fact. 'You've had a long day at school, darling,' she'd say, 'why don't you just relax instead, go and watch the TV.' I'd shake my head and insist, 'I have to learn, Mummy, I have to.' She'd give in then, spend hours with me at the kitchen table, going over and over again simple storybook words until they lodged in my mind – until those strangely mysterious scrawls known as letters began to make sense; until something clicked. I could read! It was like I'd performed a magic trick of my own. I overtook Ethan who hated reading and wouldn't dream of picking up a book of his own accord. 'It's boring,' he'd say. Not for me it wasn't. It was a lifeline.

It was coming round to Christmas again, our second in the house and the first of the new millennium. No Aunt Julia to visit this time as she and Mum were still angry with each other – a fact Mum seemed slightly dazed by as if she couldn't quite believe their feud had lasted for so long. As Mum had had us last year, Dad was supposed to have us this year, just for the day. We'd have Christmas Eve at home at least and then Boxing Day, but still I was upset.

"What are you going to do, Mum?" I asked. "Whilst we're at Dad's?"

"I'll be fine, darling, I'll watch TV and stuff myself with far too many mince pies."

"But I want to be with you."

"I know, but it's only one day and besides, we'll make Boxing Day our Christmas Day, so really you're very lucky – you'll have two Christmases!"

I didn't feel lucky.

Christmas Eve came and went – uneventfully – and on Christmas morning we were up early, washed, dressed and waiting for Dad. He never showed. We waited and waited until eventually the phone in Mum's office started ringing. She rushed to answer it.

"Oh, I see, the car won't start. Well, I could drive them to you. No? Why not? It's too late? It's not too late, it's not even noon. Paul, have you been drinking, is that what this is all about? You have haven't you? You've been drinking. Started the celebrations a bit early haven't you? Don't tell me not to raise my voice. I'll shout if I bloody well want to. You have no say in what I do. You gave up any entitlement when you walked out on me, on the kids, when you let us all down. And don't tell me not to start on that again. You've been partying all night with that girlfriend of yours and now you're so hung-over you can't even get out of bed. Talk about a mid-life crisis, you're pathetic, do you know that, a pathetic specimen of a man! And no you can't have them on Boxing Day instead. We've got plans for Boxing Day. Believe me, if I had my way you wouldn't have them at all. You don't deserve them."

I'd been standing in the hallway with my brother, listening. In my stomach a peculiar mix of emotions churned but chief amongst them was relief, I'd hated the thought of her spending Christmas Day in that house alone. Ethan, however, was a different story. Not just his face, his entire body crumpled – honestly I've never seen him look so distraught, either before or after. That's another thing that haunts me – Ethan in that moment. No boy should have his heart broken. Tears began to form in the corner of his eyes, a few of them escaping, racing down his cheeks to fall on the floor. I laid my hand on his arm and tried to comfort him but of course it was useless.

"Get off me," he yelled. Turning on his heel he ran to the staircase and raced up it.

"But Ethan what about our presents?" We could open Mum's at least.

"I don't want any presents!"

That stunned me. How could a child not want presents?

Mum eventually came out of the morning room. Her eyes were red and sore, as if she'd been crying too. Seeing me, she forced herself to brighten.

"Change of plan, love," she said. "You're staying here today, Daddy's not feeling well." She looked from left to right. "Where's your brother?"

"He's upstairs, he's crying."

"Crying? Oh, is he? I'll, erm… I'll go and see him."

"But what about our presents?" I whined again.

She only glanced at me as she walked past. "Your presents will have to wait."

* * *

We did open gifts later that day, when Mum was finally able to coax Ethan downstairs. Again it was a sombre affair. There was no tearing the paper off with eager hands, desperate to see what was inside, and no breathless excitement. In fact, Ethan had to be persuaded to open some of his – he just couldn't be bothered. One present that managed to incite a degree of enthusiasm, in me at least, was a tall rectangle, such a familiar shape. My smile faded, however, when I saw that the Barbie doll inside it was the wrong one. I had to try really hard to hide my disappointment, particularly as I'd taken pains to write on my Christmas wish list the Argos catalogue number of the one I wanted. How could Mum have got it so wrong? She'd also forgotten to buy batteries for the games we'd received so they couldn't be played with until the shops opened again – they just sat there, useless bits of plastic with no life in them. Dinner was okay but the gravy had congealed, making me feel a bit sick, and afterwards Ethan returned to his room and holed himself in there. Mum tried to entice me to a game of cards, sitting in front of a roaring log fire but her heart wasn't in it. We played a couple of rounds of snap but then she got bored, stood up, and decamped to the kitchen to start the cleaning up.

I stared into the fire for a while, enjoying the vibrant colours when I thought I saw something else in it, something that wasn't so pretty. I blinked a couple of times and peered closer. There was definitely a shape – a face, long and thin, as black as soot but with eyes that were red and its mouth kept twisting and turning, stuck in some kind of perpetual scream. At the same time as the vision I was aware of a depression on the sofa next to me. It was in the exact same spot as the first time I'd sat there, on the day we arrived. I jumped up in fright, knocking over an occasional table that had the cards on it and they scattered everywhere. Above me the light flickered ominously. My arm drew outwards and I watched in fascination as it seemed to lift of its own volition and then a hand slipped in mine. I knew what it wanted – for me to start writing. Could I disobey? Flee to the kitchen instead? I was too scared to try.

Slowly, I walked forwards, one foot in front of the other, reached the staircase and began to climb. In my bedroom, a pen and paper were laid out on the desk as they'd been laid out before. Sitting down, I picked up the pen and started to write.

Long time ago. Long time. Many of us. Many. Many. Evil. Death. House built on death. Ground soaked in death. Bad place. Bad bad place. You can't leave. Never. Every brick. The land. Lost. Some hide. Some follow. Evil. Evil. Evil.

The words became a scrawl, became unintelligible. Soon

my hand was my own again, I was able to flex my fingers and make them obey my will. I tried to read what I could. There were some words that I struggled with, but I got the gist. Believe me, I got the gist. I knew too that Mum couldn't see this, or Ethan. They were both sad enough already. I didn't want to make them sadder. I dragged my chair over to the wardrobe. Standing on it, the paper clutched in my hand, I placed it on top with the other sheet of paper I'd retrieved from the kitchen drawer. I kept them safe.

Chapter Nine

THE third Christmas we spent in that house, Aunt Julia came back. By then I'd written plenty more. I still had trouble reading some of it and had since ceased trying – as long as I wrote, the thing that forced me didn't attack – that was incentive enough. Aged seven (nearly eight), I was surviving alongside the dead, turning my face away from those that stared outwards from dark corners, acting deaf when there were knocks on walls in the dead of night or footsteps running up and down the landing that belonged to neither Ethan nor me. As for the flies, I kept batting at them, praying they wouldn't land on me whilst I was sleeping and lay a multitude of eggs.

I was beyond happy to hear that Aunt Julia was coming – that she and Mum had put an end to their stupid argument. Mum was pleased too. Despite her worries over money – which seemed to have aged her since we'd been here, with lines that I'd never noticed before now apparent on her face – she seemed lighter, and took to humming. One song in particular, or rather one hymn; the one that she had hummed the first Christmas we were here: *Silent*

Night. I preferred more jolly festive tunes. This one was too melancholy. She hummed it constantly and again it annoyed me. It annoyed the house too. I could feel its fury surge when she started but how could I tell her to stop? First, I didn't want to spoil what little happiness she possessed nowadays; and secondly, to explain that the house hated that song – *despised* it – would make her angry too. There was no point in adding to the mix.

Aunt Julia was arriving the same day as before, the day before Christmas Eve, or Christmas Eve Eve as Ethan and I used to call it in an attempt to string the holiday out, to make it another magical day. It certainly would be with Aunt Julia on the way. I couldn't wait to see her and hoped she hadn't forgotten me in the time she'd been away, but of course she hadn't. She rang the doorbell and I made sure I was there to open it, my aunt looking delighted to see me, scooping me up in her arms.

"Oh, I've missed you." She breathed the words into my ear. I didn't need to look at her face to know she was cry-ing.

When at last she put me down, Mum stepped forward and she and Aunt Julia stared at each other. They were tense moments and I wondered whether they might change their minds about such a grand reunion. A huge sigh of relief escaped me as they hugged each other instead, both of them sobbing and saying how sorry they were, that they didn't know what they'd been thinking. Ethan hung back – lurking in the shadows as so many did. Mum started to coax him forwards but Aunt Julia said it was okay, to leave it to her. She had a bag slung over her shoulder and she reached into it and brought out a big pack of jelly beans, the really expensive ones that we're rarely allowed to have

and, even better, the ones that contained all the vile flavours: smelly socks, rotten egg, canned dog food, the
works. Each nasty flavour is matched with 10 look-alike
tasty flavours and you have to take potluck when you pick
one – believe me, you don't want to get one of the 'bogus
beans', they really do taste disgusting. We'd only played
the jellybean game once before and it had been a lot of fun.
As she wriggled the box enticingly at him, I looked on en-
viously and then all envy disappeared as he broke into a
huge grin – that was like a present in itself, seeing Ethan
happy.

He came racing over, took the box, and then gave Aunt
Julia the hug that she wanted. Things were good; we'd
made them good, despite everything. Christmas 2001 was
going to be our best ever. Dad and Mum had made up too,
albeit tentatively and he was taking us out for the morning
on Christmas Eve. But it was Christmas Eve Eve as I've
said and we were eager to get Aunt Julia – who was staying
until the day after Boxing Day – all settled in. She wasn't
staying in my room this time; Mum wanted her in with
her. "Let's share, like we used to when we were kids." Ac-
cusingly, she added, "God knows, my children don't want
to anymore."

I felt like stamping my foot and crying, demanding
Aunt Julia in with me again, but somehow I knew it would
do no good, they only had eyes for each other. It was years
later that I learnt Mum and Aunt Julia had never argued
before, not even as kids. Up until Blakemort they'd always
got on.

Because Aunt Julia was coming, Mum had bought an
extra big Christmas tree and we'd made loads of
decorations to hang from its branches. Proudly we showed

them off and she made the appropriate gestures, oohing and ahhing at everything. We'd also hung up tinsel and paper chains, and popped leaves and pinecones that we'd glittered ourselves on every surface available, even the music room, which was still largely empty. It was just a big old room with glittered pinecones on the mantelpiece and a brand new windowpane. Mum had draped tinsel over the picture in the parlour too, the one that was always crooked, but every morning when we went downstairs, it would be in a heap on the floor, as if it had slid off. Eventually, we just left it there, stepping over it, with Mum citing 'subsidence' as the cause. Thankfully there were very few pictures elsewhere in the house, although there were faded patches where pictures had once hung. I remembered those in the attic; the ones turned towards the wall and a shiver ran through me.

We helped Aunt Julia unpack the small suitcase she'd brought with her, trying to ignore a much larger bag, the one with our presents in she said and therefore strictly off peeking limits. Afterwards we went downstairs for supper – Mum had made spaghetti carbonara, a family favourite, perfectly cooked because she didn't take her eyes off the saucepans for a minute. She poured wine for both her and her sister and Coca-Cola for us as we happily settled round the table to catch up on news, the children included in the conversation as much at the adults. We laughed, me perhaps more than the others, keen to replace cruel laughter with the real thing – I regarded any time we did that as a small triumph. The dinner eaten, we retired to the drawing room to sit in front of the fire to chat and play cards, me keeping my gaze carefully averted from the flames all the while, lest I see faces in them again.

The night continued to pass in a peaceful manner. No one forced me to write anything and only one fly buzzed close to my head, and even that disappeared after a while. The following day we went out with Dad and he spoiled us rotten, taking us to McDonald's (don't shoot me but it was a real favourite back then) and to an ice-cream parlour for chocolate sundaes. On the return drive to Blakemort, his presents for us bulged tantalisingly in the boot of the car, any trepidation I had at returning home outweighed by the sheer excitement of what was in them.

Dad carried the presents into the house and Mum offered to help him. They were civil to each other, even kissed each other on the cheek in greeting but Mum wasn't as relaxed as she normally was. She held herself a little taller, the smile on her face not quite reaching her eyes. Dad had been to the house before to pick us up but never lingered. This time, because Aunt Julia was there, he hung around a bit longer. Dad always liked Aunt Julia; said she was a laugh. She was civil to him too, but as she spoke her words were slightly clipped.

"My, what a lot of presents you've got them," she remarked.

"Well, they're worth it," Dad replied, ruffling Ethan's hair, who was looking up adoringly at him. "Where shall I put them, underneath the Christmas tree?"

"Might as well." It was Mum who answered. "It's late enough in the day now."

"Looks lovely in here," he said, noting the log fire. Even so, he shivered as if he was cold not warm. "Very grand isn't it?"

"I suppose, we're used to it now, it's just home."

"And Carol, have you heard from her?"

Mum looked genuinely perplexed, "No, I haven't actually. Not for a while. But, as long as the rent's paid on time she's happy, I suppose."

"I hope she's well," Dad continued.

"Yeah, me too. Erm…" Mum looked at Aunt Julia as she addressed Dad as if she needed her approval, "would you like to stay for hot chocolate? I was just about to make the kids some."

That was news to me – welcome news!

Dad hesitated too, and also glanced at Aunt Julia for approval, he must have been so nervous! "Erm… yeah, yeah, okay, that'd be lovely."

I couldn't believe my luck, we were all going to sit round the kitchen table together, Mum, Dad, Aunt Julia, Ethan and me, having hot chocolate. Could it get any better?

Mum piled the whipped cream on our drinks, the marshmallows and the sprinkles; it was like a taste of heaven. Dad deliberately gave himself a cream moustache and we all giggled to see it. Mum's smile relaxed. She seemed happy in his company and he in hers – so happy that it was hard to believe they weren't together anymore. But I refused to think about such sad things, I was simply going to pretend they were. I was getting good at that: make-believing all was well.

When Dad got up to leave even he looked sad about it. He said goodbye to us kids and then Mum walked him to the door.

"Have a good Christmas," I heard her say.

"I will, and you. It's nice that Julia's come to stay."

"It is, we feel very lucky."

"Ethan was upset by the rift between you—"

"Yes, well, that's all over now," Mum interrupted. "We're starting afresh." And then as if she couldn't resist, "Something you know all about."

There was a pause, in which I held my breath.

"I miss the kids," Dad returned, and his voice sounded like Ethan's, lost. "I miss you. Do you think—"

"No, Paul, I don't."

"No, no, of course not. Sorry, I… I didn't mean to offend you. Look, I'd better get going, Carrie will wonder where I am."

"I'm sure."

"She's nice you know. If you met her you'd like her. If the kids were allowed—"

"They're not, I'm warning you, Paul, I don't want them meeting her."

"No, okay, she makes herself scarce when they come over. Don't worry about it."

"I'm not worried, I'm just saying."

"I know, I know." Another pause. "You're always just saying."

"What's that supposed to mean?" Mum's voice had risen slightly.

"Nothing, nothing at all. Happy Christmas, Hel."

"Happy Christmas, Paul."

The door closed, not only shutting Dad out but some of the magic too.

Chapter Ten

IT'S amazing how resilient children are, how we can bounce right back. Ethan had overheard the conversation too but before he could react, Aunt Julia grabbed us both by the waist, and yelled 'It's Christmas!' in true Slade style. How could we not react positively to such enthusiasm? We whooped and we cheered and when Mum returned, she smiled to see it, the haunted look on her face quickly dissolving.

"More hot chocolate?" Aunt Julia teased.

"No, Ju, absolutely not!" Mum countered. "Not unless you want them up all night vomiting into a bucket. Come on, it's getting late, let's go upstairs, get bath time underway and then we'll pile into Ethan's room for Christmas stories."

Christmas stories? Brilliant! We'd had them last year, but they'd been so half-hearted, as everything about last Christmas was. This year they were sure to be better. I hoped for lots and lots, with Mum and Julia taking it in turns to read them.

We settled into Ethan's room, picking our way through

all the Lego on the floor – huge amounts of it, used to build tanks, cars, towers, spaceships, and castles. As Mum opened *Christmas at the Carters* we snuggled up to the adults, listening to the soothing lull of their voices. All was quiet except for that – gloriously quiet. Content, I found myself growing drowsy and fought to stay awake, not wanting to miss a moment of the story but my eyelids felt like they had weights attached.

As I drifted, I became aware of another voice alongside Mum's – faint at first, barely a whisper. I couldn't work out what it was saying, and I wasn't overly concerned, as it didn't sound threatening at all. Rather it was benign – quite benign – repeating one word over and over. Eventually, I opened my eyes to find myself in darkness. How strange. When you open your eyes the darkness fades. What was going on? Mum's voice faded too as the whispering became more insistent.

"Who's there?" I asked, my own voice an echo. "What are you saying?" I caught movement to one side and turned my head, but could see nothing. "Where's Mum?"

There was only laughter – *hissing* laughter.

"I want Mum!"

More movement, but this time it was on my other side.

Gone.

"Mum's not gone."

Dead.

"Mum's not dead!"

You.

"I'm not dead either."

Dead.

All of you.

Dead.

Dead.

Dead.

I opened my mouth to scream but no sound came out. I took a breath, tried to speak at least.

"Don't like you, don't want you."

I was so frightened I thought I was going to wet myself again. That would have been the worst thing ever – showing them how afraid I was.

"Leave me alone. Go away."

Dead.

You're dead.

All of you.

There were definitely shapes in the darkness and the more I stared the clearer they became. We were in a room – a long room and there was a mantelpiece in it – I couldn't see much more than that because of the figures but there might have been furniture too, an old piano to one side. There were so many figures, all heights and all ages, some just kids, like me, some much older, older than Mum and Dad even, ancient they looked, their clothes like no clothes I'd ever seen before. Rags. Just rags. I stared and I stared. I couldn't tear my gaze away, but oh, how I wished I could. There were so many of them, and their eyes… There was such hatred in them, as if they wanted to reach out and tear me apart. As if that would *please* them. I was going to wet myself. I knew it. They were edging closer, ever closer.

"Who are you?" It was my voice that was a whisper now. "*What* are you?"

Dead.

Dead.

Dead.

Yes, *they* were the dead, and this room, the music room, was the gathering place.

Tears sprung to my eyes. There was nothing I could do, and nowhere I could go. There didn't appear to be a door behind me anymore, it was at the far end, between two sets of windows, and there were faces against that too, pressed up against the glass. Amongst those inside was a boy, his face in shadow but spiteful nonetheless, the boy that I would scream at later in the year and who would throw me against the wall and watch me slide down it. He caught me staring and opened his mouth wide, wider still. Everyone copied him, in his thrall. What were they going to do, deafen me with screams? I waited, braced myself. There was no screaming. There were flies. Millions and millions of them I swear, pouring out of their mouths and heading towards me like a big black cloud, writhing, poisonous, wanting to consume me whole, to feast on my flesh, my blood, my bones, my *soul*.

I closed my eyes, steeled myself further and then a hand gripped mine and pulled me backwards. I fell and continued falling, all the way into wakefulness.

* * *

"Sweetheart, it's all right. It's a dream, just a dream, that's all."

Aunt Julia meant well, but it wasn't a dream she'd woken me from, it was a nightmare, a living nightmare. My sobs were uncontrollable, but thankfully my pyjama bottoms were dry – I can just imagine the fuss Ethan would have made if I'd wet myself on his bed. Mum declared me 'over-excited', said it had been a long day, but I cried some more and begged for another story, desperate for her company still. All the while Ethan rolled his eyes as if dismayed at how pathetic his sister was. Mum finished with *The Night Before Christmas,* which was another family favourite. I loved it but the opening paragraph, *'Twas the night before Christmas, when all through the house, not a creature was stirring, not even a mouse'* didn't sit well. Blakemort wasn't silent. It was stirring. It was Christmas after all, and the house hated it. I begged to sleep in Ethan's room that night and much to my surprise he didn't protest; in fact, he said it'd be okay, albeit begrudgingly. Aunt Julia smiled indulgently at his 'graciousness' and that at least seemed to please him.

"On the floor though, not in my bed. I'm not having her next to me."

On the floor was fine, we could always drag my mattress in.

Ah, that third Christmas, so quickly it deteriorated.

Miraculously, and despite my fears, a peaceful night did ensue. Mum was right about something: I was exhausted, and I slept with no further dreaming. Up early, I rushed to the window hoping for deep swathes of snow. I'd never experienced a white Christmas before, and it looked like I wasn't going to that year either, as the sun shone brightly. I closed the curtains again, crept over to Ethan, and shook him awake. The morning was spent opening our presents, which included all the things on my list, Barbie's house, Barbie's car; the works. My earlier disappointment was forgotten. I was thrilled. Mum had even made sure to get a stock of batteries in this time – lights could flash, horns could blare, it was perfect, just perfect.

Later Mum cooked dinner whilst Aunt Julia swatted flies.

"You need to get pest control in here," she commented.

"We already have," Mum replied. "Twice."

After dinner – which was delicious – Ethan suggested we set up our toys in the music room. Mum's 'no' and my 'no' were simultaneous.

"Just stay out of the music room," she ordered. "Come into the drawing room instead, where we can keep an eye on you."

Mum got the fire going, complaining of the cold again and she and Aunt Julia sat close to it, finishing the last of their wine.

After a while, still eager to please Aunt Julia, I think, and to remain in her good books, Ethan offered to make the adults a cup of tea.

Aunt Julia was surprised. "Are you sure he's okay to use the kettle, Hel?"

"Of course, Ju, it's one of his duties to keep his Mum fuelled with tea. He's ten you know, nearly eleven, not a baby."

Aunt Julia didn't look convinced.

Ethan sprang to his feet. "Do you have sugar, Aunt Julia?"

"Yes, I do, just the one thanks. But, honestly, I don't mind making—"

"Ju," Mum interrupted, "let him do it, he wants to."

Aunt Julia sat back in her chair and smiled. "That'll be lovely, Ethan. Go easy on the milk in mine though, I just have a dash."

Mum leaned across to say something to Aunt Julia and she laughed. She then stood up, straightened the skirt she was wearing and said she was popping upstairs to the bathroom. There was a toilet downstairs but we never used that one. It was ancient with one of those peculiar chain flushes that caused the water to erupt in a spectacular explosion before swirling away. Enough to put anyone off!

In her absence, Aunt Julia came to sit with me on the floor, picking up one of my dolls, remarking on how pretty she was, and toying with her hair.

When the scream came it took a moment to register.

"What the bloody hell?" Aunt Julia forced aside surprise and scrabbled to her feet. And then, her complexion grew paler. "Ethan!"

I stood too and we rushed forwards, out of the drawing room and in the direction of the kitchen. In the hallway, we heard another scream, this one coming from upstairs. Aunt Julia and I looked at each other in complete and utter bewilderment. Which way should we go? Who should we see to first? A tumbling behind us caught our attention – Mum flying down the stairs, her arms flailing and her red curls forming some kind of billowing curtain around her head.

"What the bloody hell?" Aunt Julia repeated.

I could only stare as realisation dawned. The house had been quiet in the past few days, but in its own way it was like a battery too, storing its energy, needing it to recharge so it could lash out again – and this time in the most violent of ways.

Chapter Eleven

I ran to Mum but Aunt Julia ran to Ethan in the kitchen –
both of them were still yelling, the sound punctuated with
sobs and, in Mum's case, a few choice expletives.

"Mummy!" I was yelling just as loud, terrified by the
pain that was so clearly etched on her face.

"My leg," she said in-between gasps, "my bloody leg."

It wasn't bloody but it was lying at a strange angle,
twisted like her mouth.

"Ethan," she continued, her breathing laboured.
"What's happened to Ethan?"

"I don't know," I replied pitifully.

"I must go to him…" She made to rise and then
screamed again, unable to move at all. "Oh, shit, my leg.
What the hell have I done to it?"

Tears were pouring down her face and mine – we were
both so helpless.

"Go and see what's happening to Ethan." When I failed
to move she urged me on. "Go on, Corinna. See if he's all
right."

Reluctantly I stood and crossed the hall to the kitchen.

Ethan was howling, Aunt Julia running his arm under cold water, the shock on her face reflecting my own.

"There you are," she said on sight of me. "What about Mum, how is she?"

"She... she can't move. Her leg looks funny."

"Funny?" Aunt Julia queried before adding, "Oh, Christ, oh, bloody hell, I can't believe this."

"She wants to know what's happened to Ethan."

"Ethan burnt himself using the kettle," she shook her head and looked again at his arm. "It's pretty bad."

"There was a face at the window," Ethan blurted out. "I was about to pour water in the cups when I saw this person looking in – a man, a nasty man. He was scowling at me and pointing." My brother was shaking violently as he re-called. "It was like... he *blamed* me or something. I was so scared my hand slipped."

I was stunned. Ethan had seen the man in the garden – actually seen him? The same one that I'd caught a glimpse of the day we moved in? The nightmare I'd had also came to mind. Just how many of them were out there, in the grounds surrounding the house, waiting to gain entry? It was crowded outside as well as in.

Aunt Julia turned the tap off. "I don't know if I'm doing the right thing running cold water on a burn, whether it should be cool not cold, and that water, for some reason, it's freezing. I just... I don't know." She looked towards the kitchen doorway, in the direction of the stairwell. "We need an ambulance. Here, stay with Ethan, Corinna, I'm going to see your Mum, she'll agree with me I'm sure. We need help."

We swapped stations, me looking up at my brother, his face blotchy, and his arm absolutely livid. I gulped to see it, feeling sorry for him.

"Where'd you see the man?" I asked.

He inclined his head towards the window that looked over the garden. "There. He was standing right there."

"What was he like?"

He gulped too. "He was... old."

Old? Yes, I suppose a lot of them were old – older than we can imagine.

"He's not there anymore, he's gone," I said, trying to console him. But it was a lie. As soon as I said it, I knew it was a lie. He *was* there. He was always there; a blackened soul with a mouth that swarmed flies. *Hurry up, Aunt Julia. Hurry up.* What if the man appeared again and made me pour boiling water over my arm too?

Aunt Julia rushed back in, her cheeks suffused with colour and her eyes wide. "The ambulance is on its way. Your mum's broken her leg. What with that and poor Ethan's arm, I think we're going to be at the hospital for quite a while. Come on, Ethan, out of the kitchen, let's go and wait with Mum." Briefly she glanced towards the kitchen window. "We need to stick together."

* * *

The ambulance seemed to take an age to arrive and meanwhile all four of us sat on the stairs, Aunt Julia with her arm around Mum, who looked drained, her skin ashen. I sat with Ethan on the step above, so close our arms were touching, both of us needing that comfort. The house was silent but it wouldn't fool me again. I wouldn't kid myself that the ghosts had gone away. They weren't going anywhere. It seemed to grow dark in that hall. The light was fading outside, certainly, but there should still be some pouring in through the windows from the music room, the drawing room, the parlour, and the kitchen too, but it was as if it was afraid to encroach. I started trembling again – we all were, Mum and Ethan through shock whereas Aunt Julia said she felt cold, and it was. It was very cold, but that had nothing to do with why I was shaking. No longer still, I caught movement again, a figure dashing across the hallway. I wanted to cry – so badly I wanted to cry – but what I didn't want was to add to the already considerable distress, so I bit down on my lip, so hard I'm sure I tasted the metallic tang of blood in my mouth. Despite the darkness, neither Aunt Julia nor I moved to switch the light on. We all simply sat there and let it engulf us. When I think about that moment, I liken us to four orphans caught in a storm, huddled together, at the mercy of the elements – or the elementals… an altogether more sinister force.

At last there was the sound of a siren in the distance. Aunt Julia jumped to her feet, her hand clutching her chest and breathing heavily, as though she'd been running in a race. "About time," she said as she rushed to open the door.

"Hello, love, sorry about the wait. Where are the patients?" the first paramedic asked.

"Follow me," Aunt Julia replied, explaining what had happened en route.

Mum and Ethan were whisked off to hospital in East-bourne and Aunt Julia and I followed in Mum's car, Aunt Julia complaining she hadn't driven for a while and was a bit nervous behind the wheel, but she did okay as far as I can remember. Despite my concern, I was so relieved to be away from that house, to have escaped. We had to wait such a long time to be seen but I didn't mind, the longer the better as far as I was concerned. Mum had indeed broken her leg and they were going to keep her in, Ethan too. Which meant it would just be Aunt Julia and I returning to the house. That's when I had an almighty tantrum. Right there and then, in the hospital corridor, the lighting stark above my head. I couldn't go back to Blakemort. I wouldn't!

Aunt Julia, usually so patient, was having none of it.

"We have to go back, Corinna! Stop this at once."

"No, no, no," I sobbed.

"We can't stay on the ward, they don't allow visitors overnight."

"I want Mummy!"

"Mummy's gone to have her leg fixed. But don't worry I'm here and I'll look after you. I'm sure she'll be out tomorrow... or the next day."

"I WANT MUMMY!"

"YOU CAN'T HAVE MUMMY. NOT TONIGHT!"

A nurse passed by and asked if we were all right. Aunt Julia did her best to explain but she was on the verge of tears too.

"Look, I'm not promising anything but there might be a room free on the ward where her brother is. It's for parents to stay overnight but well... you're close family, so it will be all right I'm sure. Let me go and check."

Mercifully, there *was* a room free. Aunt Julia calmed and so did I. "We've got no overnight clothes," she said, "but what does it matter? I think the main thing we need is sleep, just sleep. It'll all seem so much better in the morning."

I prayed for her words to be true, but of course they weren't. In the morning we'd have to go home, face it all over again. But that night at least there was respite.

Chapter Twelve

BOTH Mum and Ethan were released from hospital the next day and we drove home, Aunt Julia at the wheel again as Mum sat very gingerly in the front seat with her leg in plaster and Ethan sat in the back with me, admiring his bandaged hand and arm.

"That was quite a tumble you took," Aunt Julia was saying.

"Yeah, yeah, it was," agreed Mum.

"What happened exactly?"

"I… well…" Mum shook her head as if to clear an unwanted memory. "To be honest, Ju, it's all a bit of a blur."

"I'm sure it is. Where pain's concerned, the mind shuts down to protect itself."

I listened with interest to that and even slightly agreed. Perhaps that's how I'd been able to last so long in that house, because my mind had simply shut down – most of the time anyway. And if that were the case, maybe, just maybe, that's why the house had hit out at Mum and Ethan, because it wanted me to take notice, and so it would force the issue. Then again, what happened to them could be purely accidental, no evil force behind it at all. I tried so hard to convince myself of that.

Arriving home, Mum asked Aunt Julia to help her upstairs to her bedroom, as what had happened had taken its toll and she wanted to rest. Besides, she said, the painkillers she had to take were the kind that made you drowsy and right now, she could barely keep her eyes open. All of us went upstairs in the end, still feeling the need to be together, even if subconsciously, and the three of them went to her bedroom, whilst I peeled off towards mine. Making a point of leaving my door wide open, maintaining contact that way, I crossed over to my bed, sat down, and looked around. Earlier in the year I had confronted one of the spirits. It's the story I first wrote about, concerning the boy. I made a huge fuss on sensing him and got thrown against the wall for my trouble. I felt like crying out again – screaming and yelling at the silent watchers but that memory deterred me. Even so, I wanted to know why there were so many ghosts and what they wanted from us. The only answers were in the writing I was forced to do but they weren't answers as such – they were just a collection of random words, some repeated over and over again. I don't think I need to reiterate which ones at this stage. As for what else was written I needed more help in deciphering it. I was simply too young to make sense of it on my own. But who could I ask? Who could I possibly trust to ask?

There was a scraping noise above me, that strange fluttering, and at my window a fly was constantly hurling himself against it – on a death mission too. Ignoring it all, I curled up on my bed in a foetal position, like Mum, wanting only to sleep, although there seemed to be little solace in that anymore with dreams so often turning to nightmares. I could feel myself well up but I don't remember tears falling. What I remember next is Aunt Julia's voice waking me for lunch. "… and then you and Ethan can go into the garden to play for a bit, it's cold but it's not raining and well, frankly, I think the fresh air will do you both good. The heating's gone crazy again; it's stuffy in here. Not healthy, not healthy at all."

If only she knew how unhealthy it was.

I sat up just before she left the room. "Can't we come to live with you, Aunt Julia?"

She paused for a moment, her back towards me and then turned, a smile on her face but it didn't sit easy. "Darling, my flat's tiny, there isn't the room."

"We could sleep on the floor."

Aunt Julia shook her head. "It's not possible."

"But that man that Ethan saw—"

"He's gone now, he was probably just a passer-by. He'd got lost or something."

"Then why didn't he knock on the door? That's what someone lost would do, wouldn't they? Why'd he stand and stare in through the window? Why'd he point?"

"Darling, I… I don't know."

Because he wasn't a passer-by, that's why. Surely she realised that too – being located in the middle of nowhere there was really nothing to pass by.

Wanting to keep her with me, I asked another question. "Do you like it here?"

"Here?"

"In this house."

"I suppose so." Again a pause, before she asked, "Don't you?"

"I hate it."

There I'd said it – taken another chance. Now the house knew. It *knew*.

"You won't be here forever."

Wouldn't we? It felt like forever already.

"Things will change, you'll see. Stuff never stays the same."

The smile slipped from her face entirely and I was surprised to sense a glimmer of sadness within her. I realised then how little I knew about her life. Was she happy in London? Did she have a boyfriend? Would she ever get married?

"Why haven't you got children?" I asked.

Chasing the sadness away, she burst out laughing. "My, oh my, you are full of questions today!"

I shrugged my shoulders. "But why? You'd make a good mummy."

She crossed the room and came to sit by me, one arm snaking around my shoulders, pulling me close. "That's sweet of you to say so, darling. Maybe I will have children one day. I hope so. I'm just waiting to meet the right man."

That confused me.

"Is Daddy the right man for Mummy?"

She bit her lip. "He was."

"I wish they'd get back together. I lie in bed at night, wishing just that." And I did, night after night, praying; always praying.

"Oh, honey, I wish I could make it better."

"If we came to live with you it would be."

She shook her head. "You belong here."

My heart missed a beat when she said that.

* * *

After lunch, Aunt Julia was still insisting we go into the garden. Funnily enough, we'd never really explored it fully. Aside from my own reasons, it was a bit of a jungle out there, brambles and weeds spreading everywhere. Mum was never into gardening, and we certainly couldn't afford to pay anyone for its upkeep, so the brambles simply took over, their thorny spines as much of a barrier as anything unnatural.

Mum had been given lunch upstairs in her bedroom and was apparently sleeping again. Neither Ethan nor I wanted to go outside. Ethan said he felt 'too ill'.

"I know your arm is sore, Ethan—"

"And my hand!"

"And your hand," Aunt Julia conceded, "but luckily the burns were largely superficial. You're hurting but you're not ill, not in that sense. Now come on, outside, the pair of you. I'll come with you if you like. God knows I'd love some fresh air too."

There was clearly no way out of it, not unless I threw another tantrum again and frankly, I didn't have the energy. Our chairs scraping against the lino as we stood up, we followed after her, first to the lobby to get our coats and wellies on, and then out of the front door to traipse down the side path that led into the garden.

It was cold outside but Aunt Julia was right, the air was fresh – it made me realise how stale it was indoors and we breathed in big gulps of it. We stood with our backs to the music room and our faces to the bramble patch where I'd first glimpsed that figure. Because Ethan had seen him too, it made him real. What if he suddenly appeared on the path before us? I'd be terrified but at the same time relieved. If everyone could see him and realise what he was, a ghost, they'd have to believe everything I had to tell them. The more I thought about it, the more I wanted him to appear. I found myself silently begging. *Please. Please. Please.* But of course Blakemort panders to no one.

"Over here," Aunt Julia said. "There looks to be some kind of path. Come on."

Again we followed, childish curiosity winning out. Was there a path? Even Ethan looked mildly interested. She was right, there was, brick paved – a continuation of the one from the side of the house really but it had been obscured not just by brambles, but moss and lichen too, making it slippery underfoot. Aunt Julia screamed, almost fell, clinging onto some brambles to stop herself, only her leather gloves saved her hand from being ripped to pieces.

I stopped. "We shouldn't go any further. It's dangerous."

"Nonsense," she replied, "it's an adventure. Just be careful that's all."

Ethan turned to sneer at me. "Or stay here if you're too scared to follow."

Scared? I had every right to be! Even so, I'd show him and I'd be careful, as Aunt Julia had instructed. We all had to be careful.

The brambles formed a kind of hedge, effectively cutting off what lay beyond. Not that it was particularly impressive, it was just more thicket, some of it downright impenetrable in places, a shield almost. I was beginning to get bored of fighting our way through it, and tired, and cold. I hated it out there as much as I hated it indoors. I grew increasingly whiney, wanting to see Mum, for her to be helped downstairs to the drawing room so I could curl up beside her, my head in her lap. I was on the verge of turning, leaving them to their senseless exploring, I'd brave the return journey on my own, when Aunt Julia gasped.

"Look," she said, shoving her hair from her eyes, "over there, in the distance. There's some kind of enclosure."

We both looked to where she was pointing. I wasn't sure what an enclosure was but I saw a gate and a picket fence either side of it with quite a few slats missing. Behind it was a bank of trees, forested land that looked as dense as the thicket had earlier. We drew closer, our feet squelching in the mud. Inside the fence was a small circle of land, tall grass obscuring what lay there. Almost.

I'll never forget the feeling that hit me as I continued to stare, trying to make out what was being hidden and then realising, *abruptly* realising. It was horror. Pure horror. Worse than any I'd felt before. There were crosses rising up between the grasses. And strange crosses at that, not made of stone. Again they were slats of wood, crisscrossed, crudely so. We kids could have done better should we ever want to be engaged in such a macabre task. They seemed homemade. They *were* homemade. Fashioned in the home behind us? The more I looked, the more crosses I saw. There were just so many of them. It was a graveyard we'd stumbled on but not a resting place. I could sense there was no rest there.

"Oh, my God," Aunt Julia breathed. "What the hell?"

She didn't move; she seemed almost cast in stone but not Ethan. He pushed open the gate and darted inside, looking around in awe.

"Are there names on the crosses?" Aunt Julia called.

Ethan knelt down. "Erm… yeah, but just carved onto the wood. There are no dates or anything, not like you get in a proper cemetery."

'A proper cemetery.' Those words still resonate with me. This wasn't a proper cemetery. There was nothing sacrosanct about this ground.

Ethan started laughing and immediately my skin began to crawl. "How cool is this?" he was saying. "We've got a graveyard in our garden. How many kids have got a graveyard in their garden? Wait 'til I tell my friends at school."

"Ethan, I'm not sure—" Aunt Julia began but Ethan wasn't listening.

"Joseph Bastard, Edward Bastard, Jonathan Bastard, Emily Bastard, Sarah Bastard, Bastard, Bastard, Bastard – they've all got swear words for surnames!"

"No, that can't be," Aunt Julia replied. At last she went in, had to check for herself. She knelt down too, brushing aside wisps of grass so she could read. "You're right," she said, after a moment. "Every one of them has 'Bastard' after their first name, but why? What a strange thing to do."

"'Cos they're evil!" Ethan laughed. "They're bastards!"

Aunt Julia flinched. "Stop saying that word."

"But it's true. Bastard! Bastard! Bastard!" God, he was enjoying himself was Ethan, not only swearing but taunting too.

Aunt Julia stood and placed her hands on her hips. She looked furious. "Stop it, Ethan! Stop it, do you hear? I'm serious, stop saying that."

"Why? It's not a swear word," Ethan insisted, not cowered at all. "It's a surname. I can say it as much as I like!"

He continued to chant, squaring up to Aunt Julia as Mum had squared up to her during her first Christmas here. I could tell she was growing more and more angry.

"Ethan!" I called, a warning in my voice but when did he ever listen to me? I'll tell you when. Never. Nonetheless I called his name again, trying to get him to turn towards me, for the spell he was under to be broken. Because that's what it seemed like, that he was under a spell.

Another shock lay in wait. Aunt Julia's hand came out and slapped him hard across the face. That silenced him. It silenced us all. Aunt Julia was dumbstruck, as if she couldn't quite believe what she'd done.

Eventually her expression changed. She reached out and grabbed hold of Ethan's good arm. He was struggling but her hold was firm, you might even say desperate. "I'm sorry, I'm so sorry," she kept saying. "Honestly, Ethan, I don't know what came over me." He stopped struggling but only because he knew it was no use. He was no match for Aunt Julia. Her hands still on him, she knelt beside him, stared into his eyes, both an appeal and a warning in them. "Your mum's been through a lot lately, let's not, erm… tell her about this. Let's… keep it between ourselves. I'm sorry, Ethan, you know how sorry I am. I love you. Honestly I do, and it won't happen again. I promise. That… that game you want, that new racing game you've been after, for your computer, if you're a good boy from now on, I'll buy it for you. Yes, I will, honestly, it's yours, all yours. Just don't tell Mum about what happened, or about this graveyard either." She glanced only briefly at it as she said that. "It's not as if it's in your garden, not really. It's on the land behind. There's really no need to tell her. She's got a lot on her plate, your poor mum. The last thing she needs is more worry."

I'd crept closer and could see Ethan's face – at the

promise of a new racing game, he'd become sly instead of defiant. Aunt Julia knew she'd won.

She stood up, briefly hugged Ethan, and then turned to me. "Did you hear that, sweetie, we're not going to mention anything to your Mum about any of this. After all, we don't want any more bad stuff to happen do we?"

Of course we didn't, or at least *I* didn't.

"Corinna…" she prompted, "you have to promise you won't say a word."

"I promise." My voice trembled as I said it.

"Oh, good, that's good. And promises shouldn't be broken." Her smile seemed unnaturally wide. "I've got an idea, let's see how Mum is, whether she's awake yet. Perhaps she's up for a game of cards. That'll be fun, won't it, a game of cards, or Scrabble. I know how much you love Scrabble. Especially you, Corinna."

The pair of them left the circle with the crosses in it and Aunt Julia reached for my hand, pulling me towards the house, all of us complicit in keeping a secret this time.

Chapter Thirteen

SO that was our third Christmas. Finding the graveyard, the names on the crosses, Aunt Julia slapping Ethan – actually slapping him – which was just as shocking as Mum breaking her leg and Ethan burning himself. I never thought my aunt capable of such an action and inside I was reeling from it. Ethan, however, continued to look smug. I had a feeling Aunt Julia would be spoiling him a lot in the future. As promised, neither of us said anything to Mum about what we found, but perhaps we should have – perhaps that was a mistake. In a house like Blakemort, honesty is protection. I realise that now. If you keep secrets, you're playing into its hands.

Once in the house Ethan started looking at the Argos catalogue, no doubt earmarking all the goodies he could make Aunt Julia buy him. I wanted to go to Mum, but not upstairs, not in her bedroom, so I asked my aunt to bring her down.

"Of course," Aunt Julia replied, "I'll go and fetch her right now." It seems I had the power to make her do whatever I wanted as well. But she needn't have worried so much about me. If Mum found out what she'd done, the feud would start up again and God knows how long it would continue this time. I didn't want that either.

Mum came downstairs, the fire was lit, dinner was pre-pared, and we all sat on the sofas eating it – Mum's leg resting on a cushioned chair. It was soon bedtime and we were told to go and get our pyjamas on. "You're a big girl now," Mum said, looking at me, "you can wash and dress yourself. And don't skimp either. Two minutes you brush your teeth for, no less. And brush your hair too, you look like a wild child."

I got to the sink in the bathroom first but Ethan jostled me out of the way, reaching for his toothbrush. I stood slightly behind him, cross about that, about everything. When he finished I took my turn but he didn't leave the bathroom, instead he stood there and stared at me. I frowned and continued brushing, two minutes as Mum had said, wishing we had our old egg timer so I could get it exact. Still Ethan was staring.

I cut the brushing short.

"What is it, what's wrong?" I asked, confused by his sudden interest.

"I was just wondering."

"Wondering what?"

"About your name."

"My name?"

"Yeah. What it would sound like."

"Sound like?" I questioned. "Ethan, I don't know what you mean."

His lip curled as he sneered at me.

"Corinna Bastard," he said before turning and stalking off.

* * *

Crying again, I rushed downstairs. Mum hushed and soothed me, asked what was wrong, but I couldn't tell her, especially with Aunt Julia in the room, so I just said my brother was being mean again.

Mum's face fell. She looked as upset as I was. "I'll speak to him tomorrow and tell him not to be such a tease."

Tease? How easily one word can belittle such actions! He was turning out to be as cruel as the ghost boy. Talking of whom, I wondered what Bastard he was? He must be one of them. Joseph, Jonathan, Edward, one of the names that Ethan hadn't read out perhaps? I cried harder, only stopping to sip at the hot chocolate that Aunt Julia had rushed off to make me especially, trying to take comfort in its silky warm taste. It was sour though, the milk having turned again probably.

Pushing the hot chocolate aside, I refused to go back upstairs, and said I wanted to sleep on Mum's lap whilst they talked. Mum relented, not wanting to upset me further. But I didn't really sleep, I dozed, and whilst dozing I listened.

"You really don't mind staying a few more days, Ju?"

"Of course not, I'm not going to leave you in the state you're in."

"But your job—"

"Can take a back seat. Look, you need to rest, especially in the first week or so, to give that leg a chance to mend."

"Yeah, I suppose so, but it's six weeks of this I've got to look forward to."

"I can't stay that long."

Mum laughed. "Oh, I know, Ju, I wasn't suggesting. I'll get used to it, improvise; come down the stairs on my bum, that sort of thing. People have had to put up with far worse. Besides, Paul will help with the kids, I'm sure. If his girlfriend lets him."

"What a pain though. What a bloody pain."

"Literally."

They both laughed at that.

"How's the work going, Ju? You enjoying your new job?"

That was news to me. I didn't know my aunt had a new job.

"It's okay. Finance is finance isn't it, wherever you are, but at least it pays well."

Mum sighed, her hand on my hair, intermittently stroking it. "I could do with a job that pays well at the moment."

"Funny times aren't they? Hard times for some."

"Right now it's hard times all the time."

"Do you… regret, you know…?"

"Not giving Paul a second chance?"

There was silence in which Aunt Julia must have nodded.

"No." Mum's voice was firm. "I couldn't, you know… What he did, that level of betrayal, I never thought, never imagined… It just killed what was between us stone dead, for me anyway." There was another pause. "I feel bad for the kids though."

"Don't. You're doing great with them."

"I'm not so sure about that, they're not getting on great, not at all. They're always fighting, and Ethan, he's just so… miserable sometimes, depressed even."

"Ever since the break-up?"

"Yeah, and moving to Blakemort, the whole package I think. Corinna hates it here too, she never says so but I know it."

"She's said it to me."

I imagined Mum raising an eyebrow. "Oh, really, when?"

Aunt Julia told her.

"Do *you* like it here?" Aunt Julia asked Mum the exact same question I'd asked her and like Aunt Julia, she hesitated before replying

"I like that the rent's cheap," she replied at last. "That helps a great deal. I wish I could afford to rent somewhere closer to the kids' school, well… to everything really. To civilisation. We're a bit cut off here but I can't, it's as simple as that. We hardly made anything on our house, especially when it's divided between two people."

"Paul's bought though."

"Paul's bought with his girlfriend. Besides, he earns more than me." Mum shifted a bit. "Maybe this year will be better and work will pick up, so I can add to my savings."

"I hope so."

Mum must have frowned because Aunt Julia asked her what was wrong.

"Oh, nothing, nothing."

"Hel, come on, I'm your sister. You can't fool me."

"It's just… the little one hating this house, refusing to come into my bedroom, being so unsettled. You know she cries all the time, it's upsetting."

I was indignant at that – I did not cry all the time, not anymore! Did I?

"It's a big house," Aunt Julia offered, "especially when you're little – and to kids that can be scary."

"Scary? Yeah, and that man at the window, the one that shocked Ethan, that's scary too."

"Hel," – There was a wary note in Aunt Julia's voice – "have you remembered what happened when you fell? Were you panicking because you heard Ethan scream?"

"Every mum panics when they hear their kid scream."

"Yeah, I understand that but did you trip or something?"

Mum stopped stroking my hair and her whole body tensed.

"Trip? I don't know."

"What do you mean you don't know?"

I tensed too, just as much as Mum.

"Because I don't think I did trip."

"Oh?"

"It felt like I was pushed."

Part Three
The Fourth Christmas

Chapter Fourteen

"I don't understand it, I just don't understand it!"

I looked up from where I was sitting on the sofa, a book balanced in one hand. "What's the matter, Mum?"

"It's this mould. It's everywhere, absolutely everywhere. As soon as I clean it, it comes racing back. It's going to take over the whole house at this rate!"

Mum was over in the far corner, on her hands and knees, a bucket of water by her side, water that had turned black with filth. "I'm fed up of it, I really am. This house… this bloody house… what with the heating, the electrics, and the flies. God, the flies!"

"Why don't we move?" I asked the question, still hoping for a favourable answer.

"We can't, not yet. I've already explained that."

She had but not to me, to Aunt Julia, all those months ago. I could recall their conversation word for word, how she thought she'd been pushed down the stairs, that time she'd broken her leg. But then, in the next breath she'd denied it: "Ignore me. I'm getting confused. All those painkillers are addling my brain." And with that any hope I had of confiding in her faded – she didn't want to believe that something malevolent might be responsible. No one does. Who can blame them?

Mum stood up, she looked so cross I wondered if she might stamp her foot like I used to when I was younger. She didn't. She just took the bucket of water and carried it through to the kitchen, ready to change it for fresh. Weary but determined.

It was November, and we were on the run-up to Christmas again, our fourth Christmas and by now, instead of looking forward to it, *longing* for it, I was dreading it. Any childish enthusiasm successfully extinguished. Even Ethan was less bothered, not that we saw that much of Ethan anyway. After school he'd lock himself in his room, playing with yet another computer game Aunt Julia had sent him. Mum was baffled. "I can't believe how much you're spoiling him," she remarked once. They were speaking on the telephone so what my aunt's excuse was, I don't know.

Aunt Julia was planning on visiting again at Christmas even though she was now seeing someone. "It's tradition," Mum said, or at least it had become tradition since Mum had split with Dad – a show of sisterly support at a time when no one should be alone. She'd been down in the summer too, but only overnight and Mum had gone to see her on one of the rare occasions we actually stayed over at Dad's. That was one good thing about Christmas at least, Aunt Julia being here. Despite what had happened I missed her and anyway, I'd come to the conclusion that Ethan deserved that smack. I didn't blame her one bit.

It was a rainy weekend, hence Mum was cleaning – "Making a start on getting the house halfway decent for Christmas," she said. Ethan had gone out with Dad but I'd opted to stay at home with Mum, she seemed so agitated lately and again I was worried for her. It hadn't been the best of years – Mum's leg had mended but she'd not been well for a lot of it, as she'd had several colds and a cough that lingered. Ethan had been ill too, developing a mysterious rash on his stomach, like he'd been pricked with a thousand tiny needles. The doctor had said it was nothing to worry about but I began to wonder about those marks, and just who was responsible for them. I'd been okay, by and large, the odd sniffle, but Mum and Ethan were always poorly, and Ethan had missed quite a chunk of school.

Not me though. I never missed school – I had too much to learn. The book I was reading was a chapter book, aimed at much older children. I was eight (going on nine) but I could read really well and write too – of an 'excellent standard' according to my pleased teachers. I spent so much time practising both I was advanced beyond my years. With Mum busy and Ethan absent, I decided to go upstairs to my room, to look at the stash of papers I kept hidden.

Automatic writing – that's what the practice is called – I know that well enough now, a psychic ability whereby either your subconscious or something supernatural takes control to produce written matter. It can happen in either a trance or a waking state – with me it was mostly in a waking state. Skeptics claim it's *only* the subconscious mind in action and in many cases I think they're right. But there was no way my mind could conjure up any of this and from such a young age too. Besides, I could feel the hand that took hold of mine; could sense their insistence, and also lately their desperation. But of what? Of being discovered? By who exactly?

Dragging my chair over to the wardrobe, I climbed on it, ignoring how wobbly it was and the threat of it buckling beneath me. Quickly retrieving the box with the stash in it I took it over to my bed. Beforehand, I had pulled the curtains – I don't know why I did this, it just made it more private somehow as if what was outside couldn't peek in. Silly I know. I was on the second floor, but then again, there's a school of thought that suggests spirits can hover. Sillier still, there were plenty in the house itself, but somehow it just seemed safer being cocooned, so I went with those feelings, as children often do. Lifting the lid of the box, I stared at the contents, which were in a bit of a jumble I have to admit and I was momentarily cross with myself for not keeping them in the order they'd been written. But then I shrugged. What the heck. A lot of the stuff repeated itself anyway. But, and this was only very recently, the writing was becoming more sophisticated. It was as though whoever was using me as a conduit was growing with me. Either that or making better use of my enhanced skills. I started sifting through. There was always much use of the word *Death* and *Evil,* as if the writer was trying to drum it home but it didn't have to try so hard. Remembering what was above me, in the attic; in the makeshift cemetery we'd discovered; in the music room, and those that hid just out of sight, I knew well enough what was here. *Bad place.* That was repeated a lot too, often 'bad' in capital letters with an exclamation mark after it: *BAD! BAD! BAD!* I knew that too but what could I do about it?

On some pieces of paper there was nonsense scrawled, letters haphazard and shaky, as if whoever possessed me was quaking with fear. I would feel fear too, great swathes of it washing over me – emotions by proxy. And on another sheet there'd just been crosses, of all shapes and sizes. This was before we'd discovered the cemetery. I now think this was the spirit's way of telling me about it. I handled another piece of paper; one I'd read a hundred times over. *Some hide. Some don't.* Who were the ones hiding and why? Only once had I asked that question out loud and my hand had replied with one simple instruction: *Don't.*

I breathed a sigh of exasperation. As I've said before, the writing was becoming a bit more sophisticated in that different words were at last being used, not variations of the same ones. *Long ago* had been employed many times but now there was the use of the word *History* and *Key.* There were other additions too – *Danger. Leave. Go.* But most recently was the use of the word *Quick. Must be quick.* Sometimes I got the impression those words referred to me, to us as a family, and sometimes to the writer itself – they had to be quick because they feared retribution.

All this was just surmising though. I didn't know anything for sure and, at a time when I should still be playing with Barbie dolls (I didn't do that so much after that incident with the boy) I was trying to figure out the mystery of my surroundings instead; something I resented. Part of me wanted to take the box downstairs and throw it in the fire and whenever that thought popped up, I'd hear a voice in my head chanting *Do it! Do it! Do it!* And that's why I didn't because I attributed that voice to the boy who'd stepped forward. The spite in it was all too familiar.

Another thought occurred. When I'd tried to destroy the first piece of paper, rip it up, something had stopped me, a force so strong I'd likened it to a wall, bending me backwards over the bed, crushing me, warning me. But was it a warning for the greater good? Don't destroy this paper because you need it; if you want to survive you have to understand. I inhaled. Felt proud of myself for coming to that conclusion, for realising something: that there were two forces at war in Blakemort – a second one that, like me, was given to moments of boldness, who didn't just take all the house had to throw at them, who came out of hiding sometimes and fought back.

I also thought of Mum and Ethan – all that had happened to them, and wondered if they were easy targets. Those who don't believe, who won't even countenance such things, sometimes the reason for that is fear. It was hard to believe in Ethan's case because he was always so bolshie, but Mum only ever wanted to think about good things, so she'd bury her head in the sand when it came to the bad, and not confront such issues. Run away from them or, in Dad's case, let them run from her. It's not a criticism, I love my mother, but sometimes you have to meet the problems head on. Or so I reckoned – optimism returning as I began to feel braver too, like the characters I'd read about in so many books, all of whom overcame adversity by refusing to be cowed. There was a mystery surrounding me – the mystery of Blakemort – and I congratulated myself even further when I put two words together from my unseen scribe and made sudden sense of them. *History* is the *key*. I had to find out the history of the house if I was going to prove as valiant as those in fiction.

Chapter Fifteen

I rushed downstairs. Mum had gone back into the living room and was still scrubbing, still muttering. I heard her say, "How did it come to this? How did it ever come to this?"

Because you didn't stay and fight for Dad, or send that girlfriend of his packing.

With my newfound sense of knowledge I was sure she could have seen her off – won the fight. I hadn't met Carrie yet but who could compare to Mum? Despite my adoration of her, rage surged as I watched her on her hands and knees. I tried to fight it. I shouldn't be angry with her, I shouldn't! She was suffering, but then so were we. Why couldn't she have forgiven Dad? Was it really so difficult? Would I be as unforgiving when I grew up? Would I be the same as her, stubborn to a fault?

The rage in me grew fiercer as my gaze was drawn towards the fireplace. There were only blackened embers in it, but to the side was an iron poker hanging from a stand. I couldn't stop staring at it; it was as though my head was caught in a vice. All too vividly I imagined walking over to that poker and picking it up, loving the cold, hard feel of it in my hand, the sheer weight. My fingers tightened. What? It seemed I had it my hand already! I was also standing behind Mum, her back to me as she continually washed the wall, continually muttered. If she started to hum that tune… Oh, God, if she started to do that… My hand hovering for only a few moments, I hit out. There was such strength in my arm; such will. Blood spurted everywhere, like some sort of festive decoration, splattering not only walls, covering the mould, but me too – decorating me. It was on my lips and my tongue ran across them, enjoying the taste, wanting more, to gulp from the fountain that sprayed upwards, to quench a sudden, perhaps insatiable desire. Mum was on the floor, her head broken this time, not her leg; an injury she was never going to recover from.

"Oh, there you are, darling, I was wondering where you'd got to."

I was confused. Mum was speaking, but how? She was dead wasn't she? I blinked and shook my head so violently that Mum stopped what she was doing and came over to me. I hadn't moved at all. I was in the same spot!

"What's wrong? Don't do that, sweetie, you'll addle your brain."

My body was shaking too. That vision had been so real! I really thought I'd committed such a vile crime – or rather that I'd been made to – that poor Mum had been battered to death! Coming from the distance of the music room I could hear laughter, such dire amusement in it and, rather than frighten me, it strengthened my resolve. I stopped shaking my head, held back the tears, refused to give those who watched that satisfaction. Instead I looked my bemused mum straight in the eye.

"I forgot to tell you, we're doing a history project at school. We've got to pick a house and learn about the history of it." I shrugged, my manner convincingly casual, at least I hoped so. "Blakemort's old, can you help me find out all about it?"

* * *

Ethan arrived home after dinner, hugging Dad goodbye in the car and rushing in. He only said a brief hello to us but he looked furtive as if he had something to hide. Mum reckoned so too because she stared after him as he took the stairs two at a time.

"Did you enjoy your day?" she called but he didn't reply. "Oh, well," she continued, "let's presume he did."

Dad hadn't come in but then I'd seen him that morning anyway, so I wasn't really fussed. I had other things on my mind.

"Mum, when shall we make a start on my history project?"

"Your history project?" The absent-minded nature of her reply indicated she'd forgotten I'd asked.

"Yes, I mentioned it earlier."

"That's right, hmm, yes, well… I'm not sure how we really go about it to be honest. I could email Carol to see what she knows. Other than that, I imagine we go to our local record office; there must be something about Blakemort there, some house deeds, or a registry of who's lived here through the years. We could even try the Internet and see what we find on there. When does the project have to be in for?"

"Soon," I said, remembering the word *quick* and how many times it had been written.

"Let's go to my office and try the Internet first."

The Internet then wasn't quite what it is today but, as Mum said, it was worth trying. Firing up her computer, Mum typed 'Blakemort, Whitesmith' into the search bar. At first nothing happened as the computer 'thought' about it, I always used to imagine little cells like whorls spinning away inside its 'mind' when it did that. We both waited patiently – it seemed to be taking an age – Mum occasionally shivering, as it was cold, and getting colder, the temperature plummeting.

"Come on, come on," she was saying. I think she was eager to return to the fire, to warm up or try, at least.

At last the screen changed and pages upon pages of information came up but nothing to do with Blakemort. When Mum tried to click on one of the links, all it said was 'page unavailable'.

"Try again," I urged, wondering if it was another game being played – the spirits somehow manipulating our search, or rather hindering it. She made a mistake though and typed in 'Blackmort' instead. The first few links referred to company names but there, at the bottom was a link to '*The Black Death: The Greatest Catastrophe Ever.*'

"Look, Mum," I said, pointing. We'd been taught about the Black Death in school; that it had taken place during the Middle Ages and rats had been a main carrier of the disease. It had been both fascinating and awful to learn about, with drawings of people whose skin were covered in boils. So many people had died from it, more than I could comprehend, and I was saddened to think of children losing parents, and parents losing children, all the loved ones that had perished because they'd fallen ill. "Do you think that happened here too?"

Mum looked at me. "Here? Do you mean in Sussex?"

I nodded. I suppose that is what I meant. I tended to think of the Black Death as having happened mainly in London but rats got everywhere, we'd even had one in the house recently. Mum had heard a rustling in the kitchen, gone to investigate and disturbed one the 'size of a small cat' she'd said. She chased after it with a broom but it got away – disappeared to where it had come from. Of the spirits that lingered, some of them could easily have died from the plague. This was an old house, an ancient house, housing ancient souls perhaps.

Mum typed in Black Death, Sussex and called up a page. '*In the early 1330s an outbreak of the bubonic plague started in China. In October 1347, Italian merchant ships carried the plague to Italy, and then to Europe. By August 1348, the plague reached England, where it was known as the Black Death, because of black pustules forming on the skin.*' On and on she read, some of what she was saying making sense, some of it too advanced for me and which I had to reread later, as an adult, to make sense of it. '*Also in the small towns of Rye and Winchelsea are areas known as Deadman's Lane believed to be where the plague victims were buried. Other villages too, in and around Sussex, were badly affected.*' There was also a grid on this page with the title 'Villages Referenced', Mum scrolled down and sure enough Whitesmith was mentioned. There had been victims here, plenty of them. We learnt that entire Sussex villages had been either destroyed or abandoned because of the plague, villages that were mentioned in the Domesday Book but were now no more. The narrator listed them –

Upper Burnham, Old Parham, Cadlow – to name but a few. Mum read from the list and then came to an abrupt halt.

"What's the matter?" I asked.

"Upper Burnham sounds familiar."

I shrugged. "Why?"

"I… I don't know, it just does. Maybe it's similar to another village I know of. Old Parham for example, there's a village elsewhere in Sussex simply called Parham, one that's thriving I'm glad to say. In fact, it has a beautiful house open to the public, Parham House and Gardens. We visited it once but you were tiny, you wouldn't remember." She paused. "The lost villages of Sussex, it sounds so sad doesn't it?"

The way she said it, she sounded lost too. I had another question for her.

"Mum, what does the word 'mort' mean?"

"Mort?"

"It's French isn't it?" How I knew that at such a young age I'll never know, perhaps once again it had been referred to in school.

"Yes," she replied. "Yes of course it is." Again she paused. "It means death."

* * *

We stopped our search soon after, Mum said that 'morbid affairs' were side-tracking us. There was nothing specifically about our house anyway, not on the Internet, so, after promising me a trip to the local record office, she declared it bedtime.

"And like I said, I'll email Carol. She might be able to tell us something more."

On our way upstairs, Mum peeked into Ethan's room and was surprised to find him already asleep. Then she went to get ready for bed herself, whilst I brushed my teeth and got changed into pyjamas.

I'd gone to my room, got into bed and was waiting for Mum to come and say goodnight to me as she always did.

I'd pushed the door to, but it began to open, sliding against the carpet slowly, very slowly. I was puzzled. What was Mum doing? Why didn't she just come in?

"Mum?" I called.

Still the door was opening and then, with a sudden bang, it slammed against my wall, the force so intense it caused it to rebound.

I stared in amazement, wondering what had just happened. For a few seconds it remained shut and then it creaked and started to open again, just as slowly.

I held my breath, waiting for a repeat performance.

Mum appeared in the doorway, a line running deep across the bridge of her nose.

"I've remembered something," she said.

Relieved at seeing her it took a moment to ask what she'd remembered.

"That village name, the one that sounded familiar – Upper Burnham – it was Carol who mentioned it to me." She crossed the room to sit on my bed. "It'll make an interesting snippet for your project actually, come to think of it. This house is on the edge of the village of Whitesmith. But actually, Carol said, before boundaries moved, it was classified as being in another village."

Another village? I frowned, trying to make sense of what

she meant.

Mum noticed my puzzled reaction and laughed. "Yes, Blakemort originally stood in the village of Upper Burnham, so it must have been the only house that survived the plague, that wasn't abandoned, or razed to the ground."

"Razed to the ground? What does that mean?"

"It means that the majority of houses were burnt. Fire was seen as cleansing, as a means of purification, and that's what they had to do, purify the ground that had become tainted."

I was horrified. "Did they burn people too?"

"No, no, no," she shook her head, smiled again, "not whilst they were alive, of course not. But if they died from the plague then yes, I'm sure bodies were burnt, or cremated as we call it, they had to be. It was all about containing the disease you see, and stopping it from spreading." She retracted her hand and sat up straight, looking pleased with herself and expecting me to look pleased too, I think. "It's a great starting point for your project isn't it? How many children can say that, eh?"

"Say what?" I asked warily.

"That they live in a lost village."

Chapter Sixteen

THE next day was Sunday so there was no going off to the record office until the following Saturday at least. I was half relieved and half disappointed. I really didn't want to know anything else about the house, I simply wanted to leave it, but because I couldn't I had no choice but to try and find out more. I lived in a lost village – a thought that prevented me from sleeping, wondering at the significance of it.

My head was still full of it the next day as I rose from bed and made my way to the kitchen for breakfast. Ethan and Mum were already there, sitting opposite each other, Mum clutching a mug of tea in her hands and shaking slightly. I looked closer. She was definitely shaking. Her eyes were red too and something glistened on her cheek – tears. I turned towards Ethan. He was solemn, but more than that, defensive, his arms folded tightly across his chest.

I sat too. There were several cereal packets in front of me, and a pint of milk that was no doubt curdled. I gulped. Should I speak first or wait for Mum to tell me what was going on? She didn't. It was Ethan.

"Dad's getting married," he burst out.

I was incredulous. Dad was getting married? Just like that? But of course it wasn't just like that, was it? He and Mum had been divorced for a long time now, almost half my lifetime. When would I get used to that fact?

"Mum?" I said, feeling anxious because she looked so hurt. In that moment I honestly thought I'd never see her smile again. "Is Dad really getting married?"

She didn't even look at me as she replied. "Yes, Corinna, he is *really* getting married." She placed her mug down and leant towards me. "And do you know what's great? What's so damned great?"

I was surprised, was there anything great about this? I opened my mouth to reply, to ask 'what' but she started speaking again.

"They're having a Christmas wedding. They're getting married on Christmas Day!"

My mouth fell open. Dad was getting married. And it was to take place on Christmas Day?

"To his girlfriend?" I asked, not knowing what else to say.

"Of course to his bloody girlfriend!"

The one I'd never met.

It was as if Ethan had read my mind. "I've met her," he replied, his voice stuffed with defiant pride.

"When?" I asked, even more stunned. Mum had been so adamant we weren't to meet her. She didn't care how serious it was between Carrie and my dad. But now I suppose it was about as serious as it could get.

"When do you think, stupid? Yesterday."

The day I'd chosen not to go. I looked at Mum.

115

"I don't believe it," she said, shaking her head, this news another grim revelation. "I don't bloody believe it." As she stood, the chair behind her went flying, crashing to the ground. "Why didn't you tell me last night you'd met her?" she screamed.

"Because I didn't feel like it," he yelled back.

"You didn't feel like it? But you had no problem bouncing in here this morning to tell me he was getting married! Did Dad ask you to tell me, to do his dirty work?"

"He didn't say not to, he said he was going to call you today."

"And break the news, break the oh-so-wonderful news." Mum walked over to the sink, seemed to have to hold onto it for support before turning round again. "Where did you go with your father and his girlfriend yesterday, Ethan?"

"Her name's Carrie," Ethan pointed out.

"I know what her sodding name is! Tell me where you went."

"We didn't go anywhere. Dad had to pop back to his flat, we went inside, and she was there. She introduced herself and made me a milkshake. She's nice."

"She's nice because she made you a milkshake? That's all it takes. And now suddenly you can't get enough of her? She's the queen of fucking everything!"

I gasped. Mum swore, I've already mentioned that, but she'd never dropped the F-bomb before, never in front of us anyway.

"What about all the stuff I do for you?" she continued to challenge. "You never say I'm nice do you? You can barely even grunt thank you at me."

Ethan stood too. "You're just jealous 'cos Dad loves her and not you anymore."

"Don't you dare talk to me like that!"

"I will! You're stupid, just as stupid as Corinna. That's why he doesn't love you. And Carrie's nice. She's younger too and prettier."

I couldn't believe what I was hearing. Or seeing. Mum had grabbed a metal ladle and was heading towards Ethan with it. "You horrid, ungrateful little boy."

Ethan stood his ground but only for a second and then he started backing away, but slowly, the two of them involved in some sort of twisted dance. "I don't want to live with you anymore, I want to live with Dad and Carrie. I've told him that too."

Mum's eyes were so wide I thought they were going to pop.

"You…" she scrabbled for a word, seemed to struggle to find one and then it was as though she hit the jackpot, "… bastard!"

I gasped again, as did Ethan, and then he turned and ran, out of the kitchen and into the music room. *The door, he's going to open the door to the garden!*

I got up and ran too. Mum behind me.

"Don't open it!" I cried as he turned the key that had sat in the lock for years. It was rusted. Surely it was rusted. It wouldn't turn, it'd be jammed shut. But wouldn't you know it, it opened easily, far too easily, without any resistance whatsoever

As he ran in the direction of the cemetery, he left the door wide open, winter cold blasting us as more of the unseen poured in.

Chapter Seventeen

MUM was distraught, I was distraught, both of us for different reasons.

Mum also had her hand clamped over her mouth as if she couldn't quite believe the words she had uttered, the insults she'd hurled and at her own son.

"Oh, God," she kept saying. "Where do you think he's going?"

I could have told her where but I was focused on something else. Not a swarm of flies this time but a swarm of people, begging for access for so long and now being granted it. I fancied there'd be a never-ending supply of all those who had ever lived and perished in the lost village, who'd come into contact with this house and been trapped by it; some willingly, some unwillingly. After all, like attracts like, that's the belief I adhere to. In which case, evil attracts evil, fear the fearful, and horror the horrified. As my senses became overwhelmed I was caught in a vice again, my breath being extracted from me, slowly, painfully. I could neither inhale nor exhale and my vision was beginning to blur. I had to breathe. I had to! I tried so hard but it was useless. Panic gripped hard and I started shaking, more violently than I'd ever done before. I lost my balance, toppled over, with paroxysms rendering me unable to do anything but be at their mercy as they ripped through me from head to toe.

"CORINNA!" Mum screamed and fell to her knees, her hands on my shoulders, trying to calm me but the force of my spasms shook her too. She looked behind her, screamed again, but not at me – at Ethan. "COME BACK," she was saying. "HELP!"

I started to feel sick, as though I was in a washing machine on full spin. I was going to be sick, bile rising upwards and scorching my throat. If I did I might die. And that's what the house wanted wasn't it? More death.

Help me!

I was screaming it in my head.

Please someone help me! Ethan! Mum! Or the one that helped me before.

The one who'd grabbed my hand and pulled me out of that terrible nightmare.

You have to help me, please!

Rather than being sick I was choking, my tongue too big for my mouth and getting bigger, swelling up, becoming thick, impossibly thick.

I thought I could hear chanting from far off but coming closer – unintelligible words but with a rhythm to them, a diabolical rhythm.

My eyesight faded further as blackness encroached. It's strange but I could see more in this heavy-lidded darkness than when my eyes were wide open. Shapes again, human shapes, were twisting and turning, their mouths open and chanting.

Mum was still screaming for Ethan but either he couldn't hear her or he was ignoring her. In-between she was sobbing and adding her own chant to the mix, "OhmyGod, ohmyGod, ohmyGod."

Was this it? I was going to die? At aged eight my life was over. It was an appalling thought but what concerned me more was what lay in wait on the other side; figures such as the ones I imagined, whose eyes burned into the heart of me, trying to penetrate my soul, corrupt it and make it like theirs.

Legion! That was the word they were chanting! Legion. What did it mean? I'd never heard it before.

And then another voice filtered through. "Turn over, on your side."

A man's voice, but not Dad's, not anyone I knew.

"Turn over," Mum repeated the man's words, "on your side. Come on, Corinna," she cajoled, "you have to turn on your side."

Hands were helping me to roll over, not one but two pairs. As soon as I was in that position my breathing eased, only slightly at first, almost teasingly and then at last I was able to gulp, swallowing greedily. Air filled my lungs and the darkness receded. My eyelids were so heavy but I managed to open them, to turn my head slightly, to look upwards. The man towering over me was strangely tall – long, like he'd been stretched. He had on some kind of overcoat, which was dark and scratchy looking, and a white shirt with a high collar. The hat on his head was also tall, almost comical – a top hat I suppose you'd call it – but his expression was deadly serious.

"Breathe," he was saying. "Breathe."

Again Mum echoed him. "Breathe. Breathe."

I was and I continued to do so.

"That's it, that's good. Breathe."

He was crouching, I realised, but then he stood up, filling my entire vision.

"You're going to be fine," he said and Mum said the same.

Then he backed away, step by step. I tried to lift my head to stare after him but I couldn't. It was too much effort. I tried to call out but I couldn't do that either. With a suddenness that was startling, my stomach heaved, its contents rushing upwards as my body convulsed and vomit spewed from me in a torrent.

"Oh, God." It was Mum again, the stranger nowhere to be seen. "Oh, thank God, Ethan! There you are! Go into my office and call an ambulance. Don't just stand there, do it now. Quick!"

Yes, Ethan, quick! That's what I was always being told, that we had to be quick.

I think I blacked out again because I don't remember much thereafter. I only fully came to in the ambulance as I was being whisked to hospital, faces looming over me again, but kindly faces, not a man this time, but two women, dressed in clothes that were familiar at least – paramedic uniforms.

Mum was beside me too, and Ethan, Mum holding my hand and squeezing it gently every few seconds, trying to reassure me, to tell me that she was there.

I started to speak but faltered, my throat was still on fire.

"Don't, darling, it's okay," Mum pleaded. "We can talk later."

But I had to know. It was imperative.

"Who was that man?" I croaked, not even recognising

my own voice.

"What man?"

"Helped me. Strange man."

Mum looked at the paramedics, her face a mask of worry.

I tried again. "Mum, who was he? The man in the music room."

She bit down on her lip. I thought I saw a faint trace of red against the white of her teeth.

"You were dreaming, darling. No, not dreaming, hallucinating maybe."

"No."

"You were." She glanced again at the paramedics. "There was no man, sweetie, there was just you and me, and then Ethan. Only us three."

* * *

After twenty-four hours I got a clean bill of health and was able to return home. They couldn't find anything wrong with me and declared it an anomaly, a one-off. Mum looked shattered but she did her utmost to make me smile on the way home, saying we were going to make a start on decorating the house for Christmas and that Aunt Julia was coming down earlier than anticipated because we were going to have Christmas sooner due to the fact we'd be at Dad's wedding on Christmas Day.

"Are you coming to the wedding?" I asked her.

She laughed, too high-pitched to be genuine. "No, Julia and I are spending the day together. We'll be fine."

Ethan was in the back of the car, not saying a word, his

head hanging low. I wondered if he and Mum had made up. Certainly she included him in the conversation but he wasn't exactly replying with anything approaching enthusiasm – just a grunt here and there in typical Ethan style. I had a few days off school and stuck close to Mum during that time. She even indulged me by sleeping in my bedroom as I still refused to sleep in hers, and I'd lie awake and listen to her gentle snoring, all the while trying to calculate how many there were in the house besides us and where they'd fled to, the dead that had poured in through the music room door. What dark corners did they favour? How many watched at any one time? And the man who had tended to me, who was he? Not evil. He didn't look evil. Not Legion. Whatever Legion was. Was he the same person who made me write? I didn't think so. I was a sensitive and somehow I sensed that. I had so much to find out about Blakemort and it seemed such a daunting prospect for a little girl. I was tired, so tired, and Mum was tired too, exhausted. And Ethan, well… he was just Ethan.

Lying there, listening to the various sounds I'd grown used to, I felt helpless again. Whatever was at Blakemort had the power to hurt us, *physically* hurt us. That had already been demonstrated. There were forces working with us but most were against. The house itself was against us. And I'd do well not to forget that. Or let my guard down in the future and think things were going well, that they were magical. All three of us had left the house in an ambulance at varying stages since we'd moved in – the next time we might be heading straight for the morgue.

Chapter Eighteen

LEGION – I looked it up in the dictionary. It meant a vast number of people or things – a crowd, a mass, a multitude – endless. Such a definition did not inspire confidence; rather it enforced what I already knew – that there were so many here. With Mum gone from my room – she was downstairs in her office working – I sat at my desk, a clean sheet of paper in front of me, my pen poised. I daren't speak out loud, but in my mind I whispered.

Are you part of Legion?

My hand stayed where it was, no ghostly guide directing me.

If not, who are you?

Still nothing.

I'm frightened.

A confidence I would only share with my guide.

Very frightened.

Frustrated too by the enduring silence.

Are you frightened?

Slowly my hand began to move.

Quick, be quick. Legion. Bad. Evil. Possess. Be quick. Careful. Be careful.

I looked at the paper, read the words easily enough. *What is Legion?*

Death. Always. Ancient. Craft. Target. House. Alive.

My hand started to shake from side to side as the writing became more frantic.

Can't fight. Quick. Be quick. Can't win. Quick. Quick. Quick.

The pen flew out of my hand, smashed into the wall, and then flew back at me, aiming straight for my eye. I screamed, threw myself sideways off the chair, landing heavily on my left arm. It's a wonder I didn't break it. The sheet of paper crumpled into a tight ball, as if an invisible hand was squeezing it, then it burst into a ball of flame that only petered out when what was at its centre was in-cinerated. Blackened ash dropped onto the table. Terrified, I glanced upwards, to the top of my wardrobe and then wished I hadn't. Whoever it was that was with me seemed to follow the line of my eye. "Don't!" I yelled, jumping up and rushing at the wardrobe too. "Please."

But you can't plead with Legion.

The box was pushed off the top of the wardrobe, only narrowly missing me; the lid ripped off and the contents scattered. I started picking up what I could but I was pushed as I was pushed on my first day here, as Mum was pushed, straight into the wall whilst every sheet was torn into a thousand tiny pieces before my eyes, a flurry of white, the only snowstorm I'd ever seen, and covering the carpet beneath me.

A scream sounded – far away but close – as though it had travelled down a long, long tunnel, and it was filled with agony. I closed my eyes, knew what it meant.

The one that guided my hand hadn't been quick enough.

* * *

I tried to clean the mess as best I could but I didn't make a very good job of it. Tiny pieces of paper clung to the pile of the carpet, refusing to give, determined to serve as a reminder. If Mum came in and saw them, I'd have to make up some tale about what had happened, say it was me who tore it all up and take the blame. Whatever I came up with, it was the least of my problems. My problem was simply trying to survive, and not only that but to ensure my family survived alongside me.

Aunt Julia arrived a few days later. I wondered if visiting Blakemort meant she was in danger too, but I could hardly throw a tantrum and insist she stay away. I'd grown out of tantrums, or at least I was trying to. Besides which, I craved the comfort of her company. Only coming into contact with the house periodically, she seemed the antithesis of us – life infused her, whereas ours was being drained day by day.

Mum was the one who opened the door to her this time and she literally fell into her arms, relief evident in her as well.

"Oh, Julia, I'm so glad you're here, that someone's

here."

She said it as if we weren't – her own children, her flesh and blood.

Aunt Julia's face was pinched with fury. "He's a selfish bastard. Fancy getting married at Christmas."

"It's what she wanted apparently," Mum replied, her voice low too. "What she'd always dreamt of, a Christmas wedding."

"I don't care. He's got kids. It's just… selfish," she repeated.

Mum looked over her shoulder at us. "We'd better not do this now."

She'd remembered us after all.

After we'd said hello too, we went through to the kitchen. Mum said she had wine on the go, and offered Aunt Julia a glass, which she accepted. Ethan hung around begrudgingly. He'd heard the initial conversation between them and looked sullen about it. In a way I didn't blame him. A Christmas Day wedding seemed romantic to me too. I even thought I might like to do the same when I was grown up. I had visions of travelling to the church in a horse-drawn carriage through a winter white landscape, my dress a perfect meringue, my hair a mass of ringlets – a Barbie hangover if ever there was one. Even so, I could see how upset Mum was. She'd hardly eaten a thing since finding out and the weight was dropping off her. Her arms and legs were also red and sore; the rash similar to the one Ethan had developed a couple of years back. She kept scratching at her skin, making it bleed.

The fit that I'd had preoccupied Mum for a few days but then I heard her on the phone to Dad. She was having it out with him for introducing Carrie to Ethan without her consent.

"An accident?" she was saying. "A bloody convenient accident. Yes, I know they're going to have to meet her, especially now you're getting married." A pause. "Christmas Day… no, it's not just another day, Paul, it's… it's far from another day. I want them back in the evening. Are you going to drop them home? I don't see why I should have to pick them up. I've got Julia here, we'll be *trying* to enjoy ourselves."

All her words were either laced with sarcasm or sadness.

As Christmas was coming round fast, it was deemed that I meet Carrie too, spend a day with her and Dad. Ethan came along, desperate to be out of the house I think, away from Mum and Aunt Julia taking it in turns to get riled up about the forthcoming event. Dad picked us up – without Carrie – and then we met her in a restaurant in Brighton. I didn't know what I'd been expecting, from the way Ethan had spoken of her, someone young and glamorous, exotic even but she was fairly ordinary, of average height, with hair that was neither blonde nor brown but somewhere in-between and blue eyes. If anything, Mum was far more exotic, much prettier, or at least she had been up until recently, but now she was so thin, so pale, she looked like a ghost herself; this realisation startled me. I had to swallow hard, remind myself I was away from the house and to make the most of it, and that I was meeting my Dad's new girlfriend, his soon-to-be wife, 'our new step-mother' as Ethan had whispered to me one night, although that was something I'd resolved never to call her. She held out her hand and I took it, surprised by her firm grasp. It reminded me of how Mum's used to be: confident. Such a contrast to how it was now. Despite my misgivings, lunch was enjoyable – we had calamari to start with, a favourite of mine and Ethan's, margarita pizza, and a huge slab of chocolate cake. We then went for a wander in Brighton's Lanes, a network of tiny cobbled streets, home predominantly to antique shops, before tucking into an ice-cream sundae on the pier. Dad seemed relaxed, happy, and so did Carrie. They were discreet in front of us but occasionally I spied their hands brushing together, their fingers clasping.

By the time we were delivered home, I was going into a sugar-induced coma. I slept most of the way, waking as Dad's tires hit the gravel drive of home. That word – home – it conjures up such comforts, especially at Christmas. It makes you think of roaring log fires, ones without screaming faces appearing in them, of the smell of baking, cinnamon, and allspice, not the stench of something rotten, of mould that can't be eradicated. It's a sanctuary, a haven from the rest of the world, not a snare, a trap, waiting to add you to its already extensive collection.

We got out of the car and Dad kissed Ethan goodbye and told him to run along. He put a hand on my arm, indicating for me to hang back. I looked up at him, at my Dad, the man who'd left us for another woman, who was moving on and leaving us behind. Sadness overwhelmed me and it hurt, it actually hurt.

I suppose it doesn't take a psychic to be able to sense emotion.

"I'll always love you, you know," Dad whispered, his hand remaining where it was. "Carrie... she'll be an addition to our family not a replacement. Someone you can grow to love and who will grow to love you. She's really very nice you know."

I did know. I'd just spent the day with her, but even so,

she wasn't Mum.

"She won't drive a wedge between us." Dad continued. "Now that you've met her, that Mum's okay with that, it'll be different. We'll all get along."

Mum okay with us meeting Carrie? Hardly. She simply had no choice in the matter.

"Corinna?"

I kicked at a few bits of gravel. "I suppose," was all the reply I could muster.

"You do like her don't you?"

"Uh-huh."

He looked towards the house. "Do you like living here?"

That was a change of direction. He'd never asked me that question before. What could I say? How could I answer? What if the house was listening?

"It's all right." Still I was mumbling.

"Ethan seems to like it but it's a colossal old place isn't it, and I know your mum has trouble with the heating."

She did, amongst other things.

"What if… what if I helped Mum out a bit and got you a place closer to Lewes, to me and Carrie?"

That got my attention. "We could move?"

Dad held up his hands but he was smiling, glad to have fired a spark of excitement in me. "Obviously I'll have to speak to Mum, but we could work something out, I'm sure. Work's okay for me at the moment, although I know Mum's struggling a bit. If I can make things easier, it'd be good. And you're my kids. I want you closer. Lewes is nice and you go to school there anyway, it'd be handy in many ways."

I can't tell you the relief that surged through me at his words – it might have been night, but it was as though the sun had started to shine, promising a bright, new future, one in which we could be happy again. Oh, to see Mum happy, her red hair abundant instead of lank, her green eyes sparkling. I threw myself at his legs.

"Oh, Dad, that'd be great, really great. Do you promise?"

"I promise, but don't tell Mum, not just yet, let me broach the subject."

He was laughing heartily now, whilst wrapping his arms around me. I think it was the first proper hug we'd had in a long time.

Eventually I extracted myself from him and stared defiantly at the house. *Yes, we're going to leave you. We're getting out.* Dad looked too and as we did I noticed movement at one of the upstairs windows, not Mum's bedroom, that didn't overlook the front; it was in one of the spare rooms. Was that Mum? It looked like it, even though, in the darkness, everything about her was dark too, no red glint of hair, instead she was monochrome. It was Mum! I was certain of it. What was she doing, spying on us? I shrugged. I suppose it didn't matter, we had great news, and hopefully Dad would share it with her soon. I thought of lifting my hand to wave, started to but then I stopped. There was someone else in the room, standing right behind her. Aunt Julia? No, this woman didn't have sleek hair; she had short hair, shaggy like a dog's. There was no one in the house with short, shaggy hair, unless we had a visitor? As my hand reached out to hold Dad's, to find comfort in him beside me, I realised that of course we had a visitor, but not one that was living. No living visitor would be doing what she was doing: standing so close behind Mum with her hands both sides of her face and screaming.

Chapter Nineteen

CHRISTMAS Day arrived – the day of the wedding. Usually such buzz and excitement accompanies a wedding, as it's a celebration of love with two people committing to each other for the rest of their lives. Or at least they say 'I do' with that intention on the day. Of course there was no such buzz in our house – far from it. Ethan was the only one even remotely excited, as he jumped from bed early that morning and pulled me from mine, dragging me downstairs to open our presents. I always expected to see our gifts violated on Christmas morning, packages ripped into, their contents mutilated, but as I've said before, the spirits weren't that obvious.

There weren't as many presents as in previous years. Mum had warned us there wouldn't be. "You're getting bigger now, both of you, and what you want tends to cost more. Besides, you know money's tight, we'll just have to make do."

Aunt Julia had actually bought the bulk of presents, and I noticed there were several more for Ethan than there were for me. I glanced at Ethan who was looking greedily at his stash. Was it because Aunt Julia was still afraid he'd tell Mum what happened in the cemetery that day? He wasn't her favourite; I knew that, even though she'd never actually voiced those words. I was. So why was she spoiling him? I didn't know what the term was at the time but I do now – emotional blackmail. Is that what he was guilty of? Even now, I don't know if that's the case but I suspect it was. Ethan can be very manipulative when he wants to be.

The fact that Ethan's pile of presents was bigger than mine, was another reason for discord. I couldn't help but feel resentment.

Ethan strode over to the Christmas tree, its branches already brittle. He sank onto his knees, selected a present, and started to open it.

"Don't," I said. "Wait for Mum and Aunt Julia."

He shook his head. "It's not my fault if they're still asleep."

"Ethan," I continued to insist. "Mum will be cross."

"So? Mum's always cross."

"That's not fair, she's… just sad at the moment."

"She's always cross, she's always sad and she's always stupid, just like you."

"Shut up! She's not."

"Yes, she is and when Dad marries Carrie I'm going to live with them, get away from you both."

"Ethan!" I couldn't believe he'd be so mean.

His eyes on what he'd unwrapped, he whooped in delight. "Yeah! It's that new game I wanted – *Titan Run*."

"You can't leave us," I said, not caring about yet another new game. "We're a family."

"We're part of Dad's family too."

"But Mum's not well, can't you see that? Don't you

care?"

He looked at me then and I swear it wasn't his eyes looking back at me. There was a look in them I'd never seen before and that made me recoil as it had such hatred in it, such loathing. "No, I don't, not anymore."

I stood there, stunned, knowing more than ever that we had to get away – the three of us, together. This house... it was infecting him.

There was movement behind me, a sleepy-looking Mum and Aunt Julia entered the drawing room.

"I went to your rooms to wake you," Mum said, it was something she always did. "Why'd you come down first, why didn't you wake me?" Glancing at Ethan, noting the open package, she sighed. "Oh, Ethan, why did you do that? You shouldn't start without us." She asked the questions but not once did she wait or even seem to expect an answer, instead she went over to the sofa, sat on it, and stared blankly ahead. Aunt Julia offered to make hot chocolate for everyone but our lack of enthusiasm meant she didn't bother. She came and sat too.

"I suppose we'd better hurry," said Mum, her voice as detached as her gaze. "Dad's picking you up at eleven and you've got to get showered and dressed."

I opened what presents I had, taking it in turns with Ethan, me running out before him and Mum and Aunt Julia looking embarrassed about it. But by then I'd ceased caring. After we'd opened our presents, it was the turn of Mum and Aunt Julia. Dad had taken us shopping for Mum's presents and we'd bought her posh bubble bath, matching shower gel and perfume, which she smiled at but then put aside, seeming to forget about them. Aunt Julia, as well as spoiling Ethan, had spoilt Mum, with lots of expensive make-up, hair products, and a silk top in a gorgeous shade of emerald – a colour Mum used to wear a lot when she was married to Dad. Again Mum thanked her but her lacklustre manner matched mine entirely. Only Ethan loved what he got but I couldn't be glad about that, not when it was ill gained.

We had a light breakfast, no one was particularly hungry, and then we traipsed upstairs to get washed and dressed. Aunt Julia helped me to get ready, plaiting my hair into two neat braids, adjusting the sash to my fancy new dress, and making sure my shoes were pristine. Dad wasn't having a big wedding in a church or anything, Carrie had opted for a humanist ceremony, which sounded odd to me: I didn't know what on earth a humanist was back then. Held in the grounds of her parents' house, they'd invited very few people besides us, but Dad had helped us choose new outfits, and bought them as well, wanting us to do him proud.

It was ten past eleven when we heard knocking on the door.

Mum went to answer it. "You're late," she began but stopped when she saw Dad's face.

"Late? Late? I'm hardly going to be late picking up my children on the day of my wedding am I? I've been out there for an age banging on this bloody door!"

"Rubbish," Mum retaliated. "We'd have heard you if you had."

"Don't tell me it's rubbish, I've been banging, shouting, the lot. God help me, I was about to kick the damn door down! What's wrong with you? I know I got here early, but I thought you'd have them waiting by eleven at least."

"Waiting? Like good little children you mean, to be

trooped off to see their daddy marry another woman? Oh, excuse me for not pandering to your every whim."

"It's hardly pandering—"

"Yes it is. It's exactly that. You want everyone to pander to you. It's pathetic. *You're* pathetic. Poor Carrie, I pity her, I really do. What she's letting herself in for!"

"Let's not do this now—"

Still Mum wouldn't let him speak.

"Because I refused to pander to you, you went and got someone who did, didn't you? A doll, that's all you want, someone to fetch and carry for you, to be at your beck and call. I wish I could warn her. I should have thought of warning her before. I can't think why I didn't. And kids, do you plan on having more kids? Forgetting about the ones you've already got, replacing them like you replaced me."

"Helena!" It wasn't Dad who'd shouted at her; he seemed shocked by her outburst, dumbstruck. It was Aunt Julia, stepping forward and tugging on Mum's arm. "Stop. You have to stop." With her head she motioned back at us.

As though fury had released its stronghold, Mum came to. She turned to glance our way and then looked at Dad. She was so pale, so small, so bewildered. Borrowing a leaf out of my book, she burst into tears.

"I'm sorry," she said, "so sorry. I don't know what came over me."

I thought Dad was going to continue shouting but he didn't. Aunt Julia still had hold of Mum's arm and Dad reached out too.

"Look, I'm sorry, okay, for everything. I wish…" he stopped what he was saying and shook his head. "There's no point in wishing, what's done is done. I can't turn back the clock. I can't change what happened. But I want you to know that I am sorry, truly sorry. I've got regrets, plenty of them. As for kids, I've already explained this to Corinna and to Ethan too, I've no intention of replacing anyone."

Except Mum, as she'd pointed out. He'd already done that.

Dad looked at his watch. "I'm going to be late…"

"Kids, come on," it was Aunt Julia, herding us along.

Ethan sidestepped Dad and I did too, but rather than wait by his car, I stopped and turned back. Dad hadn't moved, and his hand remained on Mum's arm. Aunt Julia had stepped aside too, giving them the space to be alone. Mum was still crying and I think Dad was equally as upset. He pulled her towards him and gave her a kiss on the forehead, his lips lingering. Mum allowing them to. It was such an intimate gesture – the gesture of lovers – or lovers that had once been. Aunt Julia had tears in her eyes on seeing it and those that had gathered in mine fell.

This was a family affair. Some might say it had nothing to do with the house at all. But I disagree. Dad had moved on and was forging a new life but there was no way Mum could, not whilst we were at Blakemort. It wouldn't allow for life, let alone *new* life. I thought of Dad's words again and his offer to get us out of the house as if he sensed it was half the reason for Mum's decline.

Quick. Be quick.

Yes, we had to be, and not spend another year, another Christmas here.

But as you know, there was another Christmas to come.

Part Four
The Last Christmas

Chapter Twenty

PRIDE got in the way of escape.

"No way, absolutely no way. Just who does he think he is?"

I half suspected Mum wouldn't accept any financial help from Dad. When he spoke to her about what was on his mind, she slammed him for it, screeching – literally screeching – on the phone that she didn't need his help. She was wrong; we did, but I was nine (nearly ten) and kids don't get in the way of adult affairs. The only thing I said after the phone call – we were in the kitchen and she was slamming pots and pans and banging cupboard doors – was that it would be nice to move, words I'd uttered several times before. She just glared at me.

"Yes, it would be, wouldn't it, Corinna, but on my

terms, not his!"

I could have howled with frustration at that point but I remained mute, trying to contain my feelings as much as possible.

"Mum, that history project—"

"What history project?"

"You remember I told you, the one where we have to find out about an old house."

"That was ages ago."

"I know but—"

"Get Ethan to help you. God knows I've got enough to deal with. Another client's just cancelled on me, never got the concept drawings I sent apparently, even though I emailed *and* posted them, recorded delivery too. It was a major client. I was kind of relying on them. I'm going to have to spend precious time drumming up a bit of new business to compensate, so really any schoolwork you've got, it's Ethan or bust."

I sighed. As if Ethan would help me.

The first few months of that year – 2003 – I remember as being very dark, as the three of us detached even further from one another. That's the only way I can think of to describe it: detached. Mum was constantly holed up in her office, Ethan stayed in his bedroom, and I was either in my bedroom or in the drawing room, reading and writing or colouring in. There were no safe rooms in the house, not at all, but there were rooms I deemed less threatening, and those two were it. Stuff had happened in them certainly but in some way it seemed to be more tempered. There was no more writing, even though I sat at my desk, ready, willing, and able. But whoever had guided my hand and who had been caught that day, was still in hiding. Either that or they'd been destroyed. Nonetheless, I kept that pen and paper handy, just in case.

The black mould that Mum tried so hard to scrub away was spreading, affecting not just the drawing room, the parlour and the morning room but also our bedrooms. It was like the walls were diseased. The flies were increasing too, especially during summer, so many dead and living bodies littering windowsills; the dead ones the result of Mum and Ethan's handiwork. I couldn't bring myself to kill them despite the fact I couldn't bear them. The latent vegetarian in me coming to the fore again, I think.

The heating took to clicking on in summer too, despite Mum fiddling with the dials, turning it off even – it just kept bursting into life, old pipes relentlessly cranking up, clattering away, even screeching sometimes, as Mum had screeched.

"I must get in touch with Carol," Mum would mutter. "This house is a joke."

And I think she did but she never received any replies – something that infuriated her more. 'Why pass on an email address, if you never check the damn thing?"

Mum had taken up smoking. Apparently she used to smoke before having kids but had given it up when she got pregnant with Ethan. She was puffing her way through packet after packet, for a time I don't think I saw her without a cigarette in her hand. And that cough she had – it was getting worse. Her face becoming gaunt, skeletal even, as she snacked on cigarettes instead of food. She looked old – my young, vibrant and ever-smiling mother. She didn't smell the same, she smelt of cigarettes of course but something else too – despair? It has a smell, I swear, it's sour, it lodges in your throat, the inside of your nose, your memory, and it stays there.

But even though she was depressed, there was still a spark of the old Mum.

"If we're going to have to stay in this house," she determined, "for a while longer at least, let's make it look... more cheerful."

And we tried; we really did. Mum hauled me, and when she could persuade him, Ethan, around second hand furniture shops and antique fairs such as Ardingly, full of precious junk. We'd head out in the Volvo with Mum actually looking enthusiastic. "We're going to find a bargain today, kids. We're going to make Blakemort a palace!"

It would never be a palace, but even so, we managed to find some nice pieces of furniture and lugged them home, as well as several pictures to hang on walls, some in watercolours, others in oils. I kept steering her towards brighter paintings although she kept veering towards the dull of grey and black.

Mum was quite handy with DIY, I suppose she had to be without a man about the house and when home she busied herself positioning what we'd bought, dragging chairs over to stand on whilst she hammered nails into the walls.

"Damn," she said once, having missed the wall and hit her thumb. We ran it under cold water and she took a break whilst the pain subsided. What horrified me was that she was beginning to fill the music room with furniture and paintings, 'making it look cosy'. A vast room it could never be that, but, of course, that's not the only reason. It was already overcrowded – with the unseen. Every stick of furniture ever placed in that room sat awkwardly. In fact, every stick of furniture placed in that room never stayed in place. A wooden chair, a chaise longue, a sideboard, they were all moved back and forth, a few inches here and a few inches there, just enough to make them look out of place, untidy. Mum used to accuse us kids of moving the furniture, and when we denied it, she wouldn't be told otherwise. "Just leave off," she'd say, whilst lighting another cigarette. She'd also get annoyed that the pictures, like the one in the parlour, never hung straight but after a while she ceased caring. I suppose there's only so much you can bother about in the end.

The months passed and winter gave way to spring, to brighter, sunnier days. We did our utmost to live as a normal family and to a degree we managed it – as far as a disconnected family can. Although I'd told myself not to let my guard down I couldn't help but grow desensitised to what was going on, able to ignore figures dashing to and fro out of the corner of my eye, the sounds that I've described, the fear even. Every so often I was able to close a lid on it. Perhaps that was my mistake. I feel now that the house liked a challenge, and that it suffered boredom too, but there was patience in that boredom, time in which to devise new ways to torment. And, oh, who it tormented! I honestly think of that house as something sentient. It sits and it broods, it calculates and considers. I've told you before that there are ancient parts to the house, but what was there before? Another building? There could have been, sitting on lost ground, wretched ground, a ground caught between two worlds.

And into that world, Mum at last invited others.

Chapter Twenty-One

"I don't want a friend home for tea," I protested. In truth, I was horrified by the thought of it; for their sake, not mine.

"Don't be silly, darling, it'd be lovely to have a friend round. They could even sleep the night if it's on a Friday, you could have a pyjama party. Now won't that be fun?"

Of course, Mum had suggested before that we bring friends home for tea, and certainly there'd been visits to friends' houses after school but we lived quite a distance from Lewes, and everyone we knew lived either there or in Brighton. It just wasn't convenient for people to return visit. Something I'd been relieved about as I got to know the house better – never insisting otherwise. Mum had said, when we first moved in, that she hoped we had plenty of visitors but to be honest, besides Aunt Julia we never did. Mum used to have a wide circle of friends when we lived in Ringmer and I often wondered what had happened to them, and who had stopped bothering with whom? Of course, as a single mum it was difficult for her to go out without us, but she wore a disappointed look very quickly after we'd moved there, as if she couldn't quite believe how easily she'd been dropped. Gradually, I think she stopped any effort to make social arrangements; she grew despondent instead, even spending Saturdays whilst we were with Dad alone. But right then, at that minute, she seemed desperate to rectify the isolation in our lives, on my behalf at least. Not only was she talking about a sleepover but also throwing a birthday party for me, which was ridiculous as my birthday had already been and gone.

"Nothing wrong with having a belated event," she declared.

"I don't want it."

"Why ever not? All girls your age want a party. It's a chance to dress up, to be the centre of attention. We can hold it in the music room."

The mere thought!

"I don't want one and it's my birthday not yours."

"There's no need to be so ungrateful."

"What about Ethan?" I suggested, desperate to deflect interest. His was coming up soon.

"I've already asked and he was horrified. Just wants to stay in his room that one, playing those computer games of his. Honestly, teenage boys, it's not healthy."

Nor was this house I wanted to yell but I didn't, I just kept shaking my head, refusing to entertain the idea.

Mum paused, clearly disappointed. "Well, have a friend over then. You must have a friend over."

In the end I asked Lucy. She was the closest thing I had to a best friend. She said yes and a date was arranged. Even now I cringe to recall what happened.

It was Friday, as Mum had suggested and it was just before we broke up for the summer. Mum had picked us up from school and we'd gone into Lewes for tea afterwards, Mum perhaps worried about dishing up burnt offerings again. Lucy was in my class at school, not as shy as me, but confident with light brown hair that fell past her shoulders and a sprinkling of freckles on her nose. She was as comfortable in Mum's company as she was in mine, which impressed me. As a child I was always shy with adults I didn't know well. In the Italian restaurant just off the High Street I felt proud as she nattered away to Mum, telling her about what we were doing in school, our teacher, the forthcoming summer holidays and what she was going to do during them, holiday primarily, in France, with her parents and two younger sisters.

Mum seemed happy too. Away from the house she had some colour in her cheeks.

"Talking of school work," she said, looking from Lucy to me, "I never asked; what mark did you get for your history project?"

Lucy screwed up her nose. "What history project?"

"Erm…" I tried to interrupt but Mum was talking again.

"You had to research the history of an ancient house remember? We were going to do Blakemort, I was going to help you, but then…" she shrugged, added almost absentmindedly, "things got in the way as they often do."

"We didn't have a history project," Lucy replied.

Mum looked confused as inside I wilted. "What?"

Lucy repeated herself and Mum looked at me. "Then why did you say you did? I don't understand."

"I… erm… I wanted to find out more about the house."

"You could have just said that. Why make up something about a school project?"

"I don't know."

"You don't have to tell lies, you know," Mum added and I flinched.

"I didn't mean to lie."

"You did."

"I thought you'd take me more seriously if I said it was a school project, that's all."

"After this I don't know if I'll take you seriously again. If there's one thing I can't stand in life, it's liars."

"I'm not a liar!" I couldn't believe it. Why was she acting like this, making a point of it, going on and on? Where was the easy-going, laughing Mum I adored?

Still her eyes bored into mine. "You know what, Corinna, get over it will you? It's a house, just a bloody house. We'll live in it until Carol returns, if she ever does bother to return that is, and then we'll move. That's the only thing you need to know."

I was stunned, she'd sworn in front of my friend! Not that she seemed to realise or even care. She turned slightly, looked out of the window, but I could still see the expression on her face, it was stony. In more ways than one she was changing.

With tea over and the atmosphere strained, we drove back to Blakemort – even Lucy, ever-confident Lucy, looked a bit nervous and that was before we'd drawn up. I know I said I'd only concentrate on Christmas but what happened over the next twenty-four hours had a significant impact. It helped me to understand how dangerous the house really was, how clever, how insidious. It was a summer's day, as I've said, although approaching the house down that dark, dark lane you'd never believe it. We got home late afternoon, with the sun low in the sky. On seeing the house, Lucy perked up – was wowed by it in fact.

"You live in a mansion!" she exclaimed.

"I've told you, it's just a house," Mum corrected, her tone still offhand.

Our feet crunching against the gravel, Mum muttered about the 'bloody weeds' that were surrounding us in a circle at the front and growing ever higher. "I must do something about them," she continued. But she hadn't so far and I doubted she ever would. She just seemed to *hope* they'd go away.

Inside the house, Lucy grew even more wide-eyed. "Wow!" she kept saying, and then, "Where's your brother?" I was surprised she'd asked, that she was interested.

"He's out with Dad, but he'll be coming home soon."

"Oh, good, I like Ethan, he's fun."

Fun? Ethan? I'd never have put those two words together. Before I could protest, Lucy announced she was going to explore and was off, just like that, tearing through the house. I stood and stared. I'm not sure what I'd been expecting really, her to recoil, to be like me, to sense the wrongness of it all? But she didn't. She ran happily across the hallway, her feet clacking against floorboards this time, straight into the music room.

That's when I started running.

"Not that way—"

It was too late. She'd opened the door, gone into the garden and was waiting for me to follow.

* * *

Time seemed static as I stood in front of the music room door. Behind me, Mum had gone to the kitchen or to her office, it was always as if the house had devoured her, as if she was no more. In contrast, Lucy was in front, framed by weeds, tall plants and trees, her mouth open and one finger beckoning. "Come on," she said. "Hurry."

The last time it was open, so many had come rushing through, but all was still in that moment. I couldn't sense anything untoward, just the slightest of breezes drifting towards me, but warm, rather than that awful bone-chilling cold. I took a step forward. It would be all right, of course it would. It was just a door, a simple door.

Laughter? Was that laughter? It was, coming from Lucy. For some reason, my hesitation was amusing her. "Scaredy-cat," she was calling.

"I'm not!" I protested, determined to show her.

Forcing myself not to think anymore, not to *feel*, I continued moving, getting closer and closer. Under the lintel, time slowed even more. It was as if I'd entered a tunnel, some kind of portal, one with no summer's day waiting at the end of it, no hope at all of emergence. My feet moved faster as my breath came in short sharp gasps. I wondered whether to close my eyes, just in case someone appeared but somehow I knew that would do no good. Because that someone, that *something*, was inside me, actually inside me… maybe even the house itself. I'd swallowed it as earlier it had swallowed my mother – become a part of it, as much as the bricks, the plaster, and the lath. It had wormed its way into my bloodstream, been digested. What a thought! What a horrid, horrid thought! And not possible, surely it wasn't possible. I belonged to the house, and all because I'd passed through the music room door? Magic at work again, a black magic, darker than pitch. I was not a part of Blakemort!

I slammed against something. What was it? A wall? I heard a cry as Lucy went flying; her brown hair like a pair of eagle wings either side of her.

She landed heavily on her bottom, no longer laughing but stunned instead, beginning to cry.

"Ouch, you idiot, you stupid, stupid idiot! Why'd you do that for?"

Because I was trying to escape!

I thought it but didn't say it. Words had never seemed so futile.

Chapter Twenty-Two

ONCE I'd apologised and fussed over Lucy, she seemed to recover. She picked herself up, dusted herself down and then ran again, finding the little path that led to the cemetery, although how she did I'll never know, it was more overgrown than ever. Stamping on the brambles determinedly, she didn't appear to notice whenever one swiped at her skin and scratched it; she simply continued to drive forwards, as relentless as Aunt Julia had been. Talking of whom, I hadn't been there since the day she'd slapped Ethan, but I had to follow Lucy, I had no choice. Not only was fear lying in the pit of my stomach but resignation too.

It wasn't long before I caught sight of the picket fence. Lucy turned to me, excitement enlivening eyes that were as brown as her hair.

"This house," she said, "these woods that you back onto, they're amazing. And that, over there, is it what I think it is? A graveyard?"

"We can't go in," I said. "The surnames of everyone, it's a rude word."

"A rude word?"

"A swear word."

"What, like fuck you mean?"

I winced to hear it. We all swear, I know that, but somehow on the lips of a child, such words seem shocking.

I shook my head. "No, not that word, it's…" I swallowed. "Bastard."

"What?"

"Bastard." Repeating that word brought back the memory of Ethan standing behind me in the bathroom, staring at me, calling me Corinna Bastard.

Lucy was initially quiet and then she broke into a grin. "Cool," she said, darting forwards again.

She kicked at the gate, which swung open, readily, almost greedily. In the circle, she bent down to start reading. "Joseph Bastard, Edward Bastard…" Names I'd heard already. "And these crosses, they've got something else on them too."

"What?" I called. "Dates?" That was strange, Ethan said there weren't any.

"No, not dates, nothing like that. They're symbols, a circle with a sort of star in the middle. Don't be a baby, come and see."

Come and see? Perhaps I should. As an adult, working as a freelance psychic consultant for Ruby Davis' company, Psychic Surveys, we specialise in domestic spiritual clearance – we visit houses that are supposedly haunted and, if they are, we use psychic connection to try and persuade the grounded spirit to go to the light, or 'home' if you want to call it that; a *proper* home. Theo, another member of the Psychic Surveys team, whom I'm probably the closest to – she's like a second mother to me – has a saying: 'Knowledge is armour'. What she means is, the more you know about a situation, the better prepared you are to deal with it. At that moment, looking at my friend kneeling amongst the crosses, I knew those words to be true long before I'd heard them. I couldn't remain ignorant.

My feet like lead, I forced them to move, placing one in front of the other, my hand reaching out and pushing the gate open. It was bad in there, bad, bad, bad. As bad as it was in the attic, in the music room, in Mum's room. There were so many souls, and I got the impression that, like the woman who'd stood behind Mum screaming, they were doing the same – for all eternity. It was yet another vision that repelled me. I almost turned and walked out, but Lucy was calling me again, insisting I look.

I knelt too, in front of one of the crosses. She was right; a jagged circle was carved into each one, with some kind of a star in the middle of it. I had no idea what it was back then but somehow it seemed familiar – as if I *should* know.

Lucy reached out and touched the symbol, tracing her finger around it.

"It's spooky isn't it?" she said, not in a horrified manner, rather she was… entranced. "Have you noticed something else too?" she asked.

I shook my head. Hadn't we noticed enough?

"The crosses are strange, they're not like normal crosses are they?"

I hated having to look at them but I stared harder, wondering what she meant.

"The crisscross bit," she elaborated, 'it's quite far down. It should be higher than that." She sat back on her heels. "I don't know… it's as if they're upside down."

Upside down? She was right! That's exactly what they were – wrong, all wrong.

I stood up, one hand flying to my chest in fright. "We

need to get out of here."

Lucy looked at me, confused. "Why?"

"We just do."

Without waiting for her to comment further, I started walking towards the gate and then it occurred to me: the graveyard itself was contained within a circle, and the crosses, where they'd been planted, did they form a star shape too? Outside the picket fence, I glanced back thinking I could see a rough outline of a star inside but the tall grass obscured everything, or distorted it, whichever was more apt. I returned my gaze in the direction of Blakemort. Was it possible I could see the graveyard from inside the house, from on high perhaps, the eaves windows? That would mean venturing into the attic again and I couldn't, I just couldn't.

Lucy grabbed hold of my sleeve. "Let's go back to the house, explore inside."

I'd never seen her like this before, so excited. She was a bright girl; in fact I envied how clever she was at times, how effortlessly she grasped facts of a mathematical nature at school, whilst I struggled with the basics. She was enthusiastic certainly, with a zest for life, yet in that moment, she looked… manic.

As we returned to the house, I stopped her from going through the music room door again, by insisting we walk round the side instead so we could go in the front way. We had to knock loudly several times to get Mum's attention.

"Sorry," she said finally answering, a distracted look in her eyes, "I didn't hear you." Just like she hadn't heard Dad on the morning of his wedding. "Are you hungry?" she continued, but we weren't, we'd already eaten a big meal. Just as well, because she wandered back into her

153

office without waiting for us to reply.

Fulfilling her wishes, I showed Lucy the rest of the downstairs, her eyes still wide, only once wrinkling her nose with distaste when she saw the black mould fanning outwards on the walls in the drawing room.

"What's that?" she asked.

"Damp," I told her.

"Nasty."

It was, but it was also the least of our problems.

Climbing the stairs, her fingers trailed along the bannister. "I wish my house was like this," she said, almost breathily.

You don't. Again I didn't voice that thought.

Upstairs, I wanted to take her straight to my bedroom, but she insisted on peeking in all of them, lingering mainly in Ethan's, which she declared 'cool'. We stood just in the doorway and I didn't think it was cool at all. It was unbelievably messy, with his clothes on the floor where he'd dropped them, his bed unmade. But worst of all was the smell. I couldn't quite place it, but it was pungent, offensive even. Not that wide-eyed Lucy seemed to notice, she was so in awe of him. Why hadn't Mum been in to clean Ethan's room, or at least ordered him to? Come to think of it, she hadn't been in to tidy mine recently. I tried to think of the last time and realised I couldn't.

I wanted to escape Ethan's room, the whole unsavoury feel of it. "Come on," I urged.

Lucy seemed happy enough to follow me and then she caught a glimpse of another stairway, the one that hid itself away.

"What's this?" she said, going towards it.

As I'd done when she'd hurtled towards the music room

door, I yelled, "Don't!"

Again she ignored me. Standing at the bottom of those narrow stairs, she stared upwards. "It's the stairs to the attic!"

I groaned. Why, oh why, did this house fascinate her? I'm sorry to say I began doubting myself in that moment. Believing that perhaps I was just too imaginative a child. There was nothing wrong with Blakemort, absolutely nothing. It was normal. I wasn't. I was *abnormal.* And then I shook my head. The graveyard... I didn't make that up. That was real enough.

"Let's go on up," she said, her foot already on the lowest tread.

"Let's just go to my bedroom, we can play with Barbie—"

She sniggered. "I don't play with Barbie anymore. No one does, stupid."

Oh, that word! Ethan used it all the time and now Lucy.

I strode forward and pushed past her. "Okay, okay, come on then, let's go. Let's do what you want to do and explore the attic, the boring old attic."

But it hadn't been boring before. I only hoped it would be this time. And, as kids do, I searched for a positive. At the very least I might catch a glimpse of the graveyard – to see if it really did resemble the shape on the crosses. As I've said, I hadn't been up there since that first year having carefully avoided it, whereas Ethan just didn't seem bothered by it. Mum never suggested it either, but why would she? People don't hang about in such places. But some things do. Some prefer them.

As it had been before, the door was slightly ajar. Pushing it open, I did as Ethan had and groped for the light pull, half expecting something to grab my hand and drag me in. I tugged and light of sorts relieved the gloom.

"It's packed full of stuff!" said Lucy.

It was. Dead stuff.

She walked over to the box that Ethan had delved into and gingerly looked inside. "Be good if we had a torch," she said, "it's hard to see stuff properly."

"Come over here," I said steering her away from it, from any photos that lay spoiled at her feet, that I'd urinated on in terror. "There's loads of clothes over here, just lying around."

Despite myself I was intrigued. Could they be dressing up clothes? They certainly looked like it. There were masks as well as cloaks, black in colour, and shifts, bundles and bundles of them. One mask in particular caught my attention, its nose was in the shape of a beak and, like everything else in that house, it smelt rank, but this time in an earthy sort of way, herbal almost, like the oregano Mum used in her bolognaise but a hundred times worse; nothing appetising about it at all. Whilst Lucy held a cloak up, I shifted over to one of the windows in an attempt to spot the graveyard.

"What do you think?" Lucy said, having draped herself in the garment.

"Hmm, cool," I said, not looking.

"I'll put one of the masks on too," she added.

"Yeah, sure, it'll be funny."

Where was it? Over to the left a bit, perhaps a bit more to the right, through that clump of trees that stood like sentinels. There it was! Tiny now but the picket fence gave it depth at least. I squinted, peered harder. Yes, the crosses did form some sort of shape but still the grass obscured them, it could be a star, it could well be a star. If only I could have magnified the whole thing just to be sure. Re-adjusting my eyesight, I blinked several times, looked to the left slightly, and that's when I saw what was engraved on the wood of the windowsill: more of those symbols – the circle and the cross – other marks too, letters, but none that I recognised. It was an alphabet of another kind. I reached up to trace them as Lucy had traced them outside, felt the roughness of the carving, wondered if splinters might lodge in my fingertips and then I screamed as something flew at me, my hand striking out instead.

"Lucy!" I said, hardly believing what I'd done. I hadn't realised it was her; I thought it was the fluttering thing that had attacked me before. Certainly, all I'd seen was something black in the corner of my eye but that had been the cloak she wore, the whiteness of her face covered by something black too, a mask. I rushed towards her. "I'm sorry, I didn't mean—"

"That's the second time you've hit me!"

"I didn't mean to, and besides, the first time I bumped into you, I didn't hit you."

I was in danger of gabbling so I shut up, reached out a hand, but she slapped it away.

"Don't touch me. Don't you dare touch me!"

"Lucy, I'm sorry." I was desperate for her to calm down. Anger in that house only incited more. "Let me help you."

"No!"

She got herself up, struggling slightly, before standing right in front of me. In the black cloak and the black mask she looked almost inhuman; a shape, a shadow, or something that belonged to the shadows, that should never see the daylight.

"You're stupid that's what you are, and violent. Wait 'til I tell my Mum what you've done, when I tell *your* Mum, that we were playing, that you attacked me."

Again I was stunned. How could she say such words to me, threaten me like that? I hadn't hit her, not deliberately and we weren't playing, we were exploring, something I didn't want to do, which she *made* me do. Anger rose in me too.

"Don't you dare tell my mum," I warned.

"I will, and you'll be in trouble, big trouble."

I took a step forwards. "You'd better not, I'm warning you."

"Or you'll do what? You're stupid, you can't do anything."

"Stop calling me stupid."

"I won't, because that's what you are. Stupid, stupid, stupid!"

"Stop it!"

"Stupid, stupid, stupid!" She repeated it on a loop, each word a blow too.

I was breathing so hard, my chest rising up and down as fury began to blind me. Often it's described as a red mist and I think that's accurate enough. Certainly it seemed to obscure my vision. In front of me all was hazy, the black of her and the black of the others blending, the excitement, the *hatred* in the air palpable. My hands bunched into fists as the others formed a circle around us – always a circle – as they closed us in and trapped us. Couldn't she sense them too? Was she really oblivious? She must have been, and stupid too, despite hurling that word at me.

Go on. Kill her!

It was a voice in my ear. I turned my head abruptly but

there was no one there.

Kill her!

The voice in my other ear now, but again disembodied.

KILL HER!

It was screaming, the sound a knife blade, as sharp, and as piercing.

Or we'll kill you!

One hand rising, I drew it back. It was down to her or me. Only one of us would survive. The cloak and the mask helped, as it didn't look like Lucy. It didn't look like anyone. Faceless and formless, she was easier to kill… to kill… to kill…

I gasped. What was I thinking? She was supposed to be my friend, my best friend.

Lucy had a change of heart too. She stopped chanting, took off her mask, her expression as confused as mine I'm sure.

"Corinna, I'm—"

As if my fist had a will of its own, it drew back and then forwards, sending Lucy flying for the third time.

Chapter Twenty-Three

NEEDLESS to say, Lucy didn't stay that night, she ran from the attic, tripping over the black cloak on several occasions and nearly falling again, screaming for my mother. I ran after her, shaking violently, every now and then glancing at my right hand, as if it didn't belong to me – and it hadn't, not during the moment it came into contact with Lucy's face. It wasn't my fault, it wasn't! Not that Lucy would believe me, or Mum, or Lucy's Mum. She was horrified when she came racing over to pick Lucy up and Mum bore the full brunt of her anger instead of me – ordering me in the drawing room and closing the door. Left me in there to listen, to them, and to the laughter that echoed around. Had the boy, that spiteful boy, that *evil* boy, grabbed hold of my fist? Was he the one responsible? There were just so many of them it was impossible to tell.

The following week there were only three days left at school before term was finally over and Mum kept me home, insisting it was the best thing to do, that the fuss over what had happened would die down if I stayed away. Ethan had been furious that he'd had to go in when I didn't, had looked at me as if I'd choreographed the whole thing, but there was one thing he didn't do: he didn't call me stupid.

We didn't go away that year, there was no way we could afford to, and eventually summer gave way to autumn and the start of a new school year. Lucy hadn't forgotten my supposed treatment of her and made sure several others turned their backs on me too. I spent so many playtimes on my own, and no one ever visited the house again, nor was I invited to their houses, not anymore. It was just the routine of school, home and going out with Dad on a Saturday. That's what the house had done – it had isolated us. How I longed for Aunt Julia's visits at least.

"She is coming for Christmas, isn't she?" I checked with Mum one afternoon when we were in the kitchen. Mum was attempting to make scones, but she'd already burnt the first batch. "Mum," I said again, having to prompt her, as she kept a strict eye on the timing of the second.

"Hmm, yes, yes, I think so. If we're still here that is."

I could hardly believe my ears. "What do you mean if we're still here?"

Finally she looked at me. "Well, I'm not sure I can face another winter, you know? Freezing one minute, boiling the next. And it's too far out. I want to be closer to life."

Closer to life? Me too! I wanted nothing more.

Barely able to contain my excitement, I started jumping up and down. "When can we move? When? When? When?"

Mum laughed and as she did I was struck by how lovely it was to see a genuine smile light up her face, it had been a long time since I'd seen that, too long. Retrieving the scones from the oven, that batch only slightly better than the first, despite her diligence, Mum affectionately told me to calm down. "We can't just move in an instant, it doesn't work like that. I've got to give Carol notice. It's only polite. Then we have to start looking. Well, I say start, but to be honest I've been looking already."

"I thought we couldn't afford to move," I said, worried again.

Mum averted her gaze at this and I had to prompt her again for an answer.

"I've accepted help from your dad," she confided, before giving a defiant shrug. "I don't see why not. I look after his children so it's for your benefit as well as mine." She looked around her. "I just don't think it's good for us being here that's all."

My heart skipped a beat. She'd noticed! I wasn't alone. My relief was incredible. It seemed to flood right through me. *But don't let the house know.* Quickly the words formed in my mind. *Keep your plans as secret as possible.* But have you tried keeping things from the walls that surround you, the very air that you breathe? It's impossible. That was something I didn't want to think about. All I wanted to do was to soak up what she'd told me and to dream of a future without Blakemort in it.

Mum called Ethan and we sat at the kitchen table with a pot of tea, the not-so-burnt scones and the jam and the cream. This was our dinner, and, in that moment, as far as I was concerned, it was the dinner of kings and queens! Covering one half of my scone with butter, I reached for the jam and piled that on too, but as my knife dipped into the clotted cream, I saw it congeal before my eyes.

Mum noticed too. "What the heck? I bought that cream yesterday, checked the sell by date specially and it was fine.

God, I don't know, it's just…" She shook her head, started agitating at her lip. "The sooner Carol replies to my emails the better."

After tea, I followed Ethan upstairs. Mum had said she'd told him earlier about her plans, although it wasn't within my earshot, and I wanted to gauge his reaction. Ethan stopped just shy of opening his door and turned to me. He was nearly thirteen now and I suppose I could understand the effect he'd had on Lucy earlier in the year. His face was nice enough; he had big eyes, and thick dark hair. He'd also grown recently, he was head and shoulders above me, and his arms were strong, despite doing nothing but sitting in front of his computer, playing endless games. What marred his looks slightly was a rash of spots along his jaw-line. They reminded me of the rash he'd once had – tiny dents and holes, as if someone had stuck pins into him.

"It's great news, isn't it, Ethan, about moving?" I kept my voice deliberately low.

Ethan looked far from impressed. "Not really, I like it here."

"Like what exactly?" I was curious to know.

"It's big, big enough so I don't have to bump into you anyway."

I ignored his comment and carried on, "We might go to live in Lewes, or in Brighton, Mum hasn't decided yet." Wherever it was I longed for a small house, terraced too, with shops close by, cars and people – ordinary people.

"Whatever…" He really wasn't giving much away. "I'll believe it when I see it."

He turned his back on me and went to open his bed-room door.

"What do you mean you'll believe it when you see it?

Don't you believe Mum?"

He shrugged.

"Ethan?"

"Mum's different isn't she? She's not the same any-more."

Nor are you! I wanted to shout.

"It's this house," I said at last, hardly daring to believe my own bravery. "It's because of the house."

He turned his head to look me in the eye. I held his gaze, refusing to be intimidated. *Go on say it. Call me stu-pid. I dare you.*

He didn't, he just sneered some more and then entered his den, leaving me alone on the landing with the house bristling around me.

* * *

It was later in the month of October that I went into Ethan's room, not on Halloween, although Halloween would have certainly suited the occasion. I don't know where he'd gone – probably to a friend's or something – and I was on my way to the bathroom when a familiar smell assailed me, drifting out of his room, vaporous al-most and filling the air. What was going on behind closed doors? If Mum wasn't curious, I was. I decided to take a peek. He'd never know.

Despite Mum being downstairs, I tiptoed across. Silly really, there was no reason not to walk boldly over. My breathing slightly ragged, I pushed open the door. That smell... it far surpassed that of his trainers and, believe me, they were bad enough. My eyes started watering, and I al-most choked. How come Mum hadn't noticed this? His bedroom was right next to hers.

I slipped inside, not closing the door entirely behind me, but leaving it open just a crack. The curtains were closed on an already darkening night; I suspected those curtains were never opened, that Ethan always shut the light out. Groping for the light switch, I finally found it; the light was the same sickly yellow as in the attic, leaving so much gloom. His room was as untidy as I'd expected it to be, clothes and shoes everywhere, computer games strewn across the surface of his desk, which already vied for space with a computer and a small TV. He had shelves on the walls too, books, *Star Wars* figures and packs of Top Trumps adorning them. Long gone was the Lego, taken to some charity shop for someone else to play with. Tentatively, I made my way over to the desk and opened various drawers, which were stuffed full with socks, underwear, t-shirts, more computer games, and a homework book. Selecting the latter, I flicked through it, although it didn't contain much, but then Ethan wasn't keen on homework and would do anything he could to get out of it. Mum used to make him, but I guess she didn't anymore.

So all was normal. What wasn't? I scanned shelves again, the floor, then went over to the curtains, to move them aside so I could check the windowsill. Puzzled, I stopped to think. If he had something to hide, something rotten, where would it be? My eyes rested on the wardrobe in the far corner. Of course! After all, that's where I'd hidden something too.

I took a deep breath and walked over, the light flickering above me as I moved. A warning? It certainly felt like one. Standing in front of the wardrobe, it was a solid piece of furniture, already in situ when we arrived, the dark wood giving it an old-fashioned appearance. It had a thin piece of mirror running down the middle of it, tarnished slightly with brown spots – reminding me of the kind you sometimes see on the back of old people's hands. I caught sight of my reflection, something I was wary of doing. I always hated looking at myself in mirrors in that house, wondering if when I turned away, my reflection would still be staring outwards.

I reached out a hand, as did my mirror image, turned the handle, and heard the click as it yielded. The smell as good as flew at me. Gagging, I lifted both hands to my face in a bid to protect myself. And then my hands dropped as my mouth fell open. There were no clothes in the wardrobe, none at all. But it was far from empty.

Ethan had been in the attic! Clearly he'd been there on several occasions. What was up there: the insects forever trapped in glass weights, the pinned butterflies, a few of the photographs – the dead things basically – he'd looted them. Not only were they in his wardrobe, he'd added to them a collection of his own: flies. There were so many flies, lying in heaps, their bodies rotting. There were the carcasses of larger insects too – beetles, centipedes and spiders. He must have spent ages rummaging in the garden for them. And something else, something I had to force myself to look at – a field mouse, a tiny little field mouse, staked, as the butterflies were staked, one half of it putrefying. I could hardly tear my gaze away, not because I was fascinated but because I was trying to tell myself that Ethan didn't do this, that he didn't know it was there and that someone else was responsible. Ethan might be a pain, he might be nasty to me, but he was still my brother and I loved him. I didn't want him to be capable of this. I was about to turn, get out, when I saw something in the wardrobe move. What was it? What could possibly live amongst so many dead? And if it was alive, could I help it? Release it from my brother and his tyranny? I leaned forward slightly. Yes, there was something in there, beneath layers of flies, struggling to get out. Dare I find a stick... something I could use to poke around a bit? There was no way I was touching anything with my hands. I looked behind me; the best thing I could find was a pen. It was no good. I needed something longer. What else, what else? A ruler! That'd do – at least it meant I didn't have to put my hand inside the wardrobe, I could just hold it at the tip. I didn't want to do it, I really didn't, but I happen to believe all creatures are sacred, that we should help anything in peril. Even so, I hoped it wasn't a spider, I'd never killed one, but the big ones frightened me.

I started moving the ruler, shifting the vile contents, trying to ignore the aroma of death and decay. Where was it, the thing I'd seen moving? Had I imagined it, with my mind playing tricks on me? But no, I'd seen rippling and heaving, there was something there. Reaching further in, it was as if the ruler started moving of its own accord, left to right, only slightly at first, imperceptibly, but then with more force.

Let it go. Turn and run.

Those were my instructions to myself and I was about to obey them when it seemed as if something crawled up the ruler – yes, crawled – and closed itself around my hand instead. I screamed, started pulling back in earnest now.

"Let go of me! Let go of me!"

What was it that had me in its clasp? Nothing that was remotely human. It was insectile, many legged, and it

167

wanted to impale me too.

"No!" I continued to scream. "No! No! No!"

As much as it pulled, I pulled too, my other hand flat against the wardrobe, in an attempt to give myself extra leverage. I was failing, drastically. This thing was much stronger than me, I was going to fall into the wardrobe, be shut in, and left to fester.

"Help! Someone help me!"

But Mum was downstairs, she'd never be able to hear me – the house would make sure of it.

"Help!" My voice was hoarse; soon I wouldn't be able to scream at all. "Help!"

My call was answered but cruelly. I was thrown back, hitting my head against one of the drawers on Ethan's desk and the wardrobe door slammed shut. But the horrors weren't over, not by a long shot. There was an image in the wardrobe mirror: me. I was standing hand in hand with someone. A boy? It looked like it.

And we were laughing.

Chapter Twenty-Four

OF course I wanted to go downstairs straightway and tell Mum what I'd seen and I proposed to do just that. Despite my aching head, I got myself up, ran out of Ethan's room, turned left on the landing and at the top of the stairs I skidded to a halt. What would the repercussions be if I told Mum? How badly would Ethan get into trouble? What if it was really badly and she sent him to live with Dad whilst we waited to leave? There'd be just the two of us left then. Another thought: what if she told the police? Young as I was, I thought that was possible. He'd get taken away, put in prison. For how long? It could be months, years even. I couldn't tell her. Besides, it would feel like snitching. *Telltale! Tell-tale!* I could imagine Ethan yelling it at me. I had one option and that was to encourage Mum to leave – she was our only hope, our means of escape. All she had to do was get in touch with Carol first.

The weeks passed, I kept away from Ethan, certainly away from his room. I still found it so hard to believe that he was capable of what I'd seen. I considered talking to him about it, but quickly thought again. He wouldn't talk to me. As for Carol, why wasn't she replying to Mum's emails? Was it really so vital that she did? Couldn't we just leave anyway? Mum was adamant we couldn't. "It's not fair to do that, besides I haven't found the ideal place for us yet."

As far as I was concerned the gutter was preferable to Blakemort. I tried to talk to Dad too, but he just told me not to worry, that Mum was sorting it. "It can be hard to keep up with affairs back home when you're travelling, but I'm sure Carol will be in touch soon. Perhaps it's best to wait until after Christmas to contact her."

He said what I dreaded hearing: that we had to spend another Christmas here.

Mum was looking forward to seeing Aunt Julia again. Apparently she'd split up with her boyfriend and was a bit down about it. "She really thought he was the one," Mum told me. "It's funny how we can be so wrong about people." It was; about people, houses, and those closest to us. I was still so worried about Ethan.

"Mum, Ethan's room…" I began.

We were sitting on the sofa, trying to watch TV but the signal kept dipping in and out, making it close to impossible.

"What about it?" she asked.

"Have you been in there lately?"

She laughed. Well, it was more of a snort really. "I daren't. Teenage boys rooms are something to be feared, darling." If only she knew how much. "No," she continued, "Ethan's a big boy now, he can clean his own room. I don't see why I should do it. I do enough around here. If he wants to live in a pig sty, let him."

Christmas was drawing closer and there was still no

word from Carol. Mum wanted to put the decorations up and so we went to nearby Wilderness Woods to buy our tree, hoping for one that wasn't quite as forlorn as last year. It certainly looked abundant as we dragged it through the hallway, pine needles littering the floor although their clean almost antiseptic smell failed to penetrate. Once positioned upright, the tree's glamour decreased dramatically. Nonetheless, Mum retrieved the box of Christmas decorations that she kept in one of the spare rooms and we began to hang ornaments from its branches, Ethan dropping one of her prized baubles, made of Murano glass, one that Dad had bought her whilst they were on honeymoon in Venice. There were tears in her eyes as she picked up the jagged pieces.

Again we adorned picture frames with tinsel but, as soon as our backs were turned, they slid off. Mum bent to retrieve one of the garlands and then frowned.

"What's the matter?" I asked.

"It's nothing, it's just… how strange. Look at this picture here, it appears as if the canvas is cracking, distorting the entire thing, making it look wavy instead." She lifted a finger and scraped at the surface with her nail. "How odd, the paint is flaking too." Examining other pictures, she found the same thing. "It must be something to do with the heating," she surmised, looking for excuses again. "That bloody heating!"

"Perhaps we shouldn't bother with the tinsel," I suggested.

She nodded. "I think you're right, we shouldn't bother anymore."

Mum went into the kitchen to do some baking instead, humming that tune of hers. Later, when I went in to find her, she'd done no baking at all. Instead she was sitting, smoking a cigarette, shards of Murano glass lying on the table in front of her.

* * *

Aunt Julia was due down on Christmas Eve Eve (as we called it). Christmas Eve we were spending with Dad and Carrie, to be dropped home that same evening. I was dreading the big day, absolutely dreading it, hating the Christmas tree in the drawing room that looked so out of place, a season that should be happy but which, at Blakemort, never was. And none of it was helped by Dad's news – Carrie was pregnant, by over three months. We had a half-brother or sister on the way. Ethan was pleased, even I was secretly pleased, but Mum was shocked, truly shocked. As she broke the news to us she was trembling. When Aunt Julia arrived a few hours later she must have been informed too because she bypassed us and went straight to Mum, the two of them disappearing to talk. Whilst they did I went into Mum's office, sat at the computer and opened up her email account, I wanted to see if it was true, if she'd really been emailing Carol. I'm sorry to admit it but I thought she could be lying, actually lying, that she'd been as seduced by this house as Ethan was. It took me a fair bit of scrolling but sure enough she'd sent various emails, latterly typing, *'What's wrong, Carol? Is something wrong? I really need to hear from you. I hope you're having the time of your life and I understand you're busy, but it's been so long. Please, just let me know that you're okay.'*

For some reason, those words caused alarm. *'What's wrong, Carol?'* I hadn't thought anything to be wrong before. As Dad had said, she was simply preoccupied with her travels, but what if she wasn't? What if something *had* happened to her? Would that mean we'd be stuck here, that we'd never escape?

My hand started typing a fresh email – I couldn't stop myself. *'What's wrong, Carol? What's wrong, Carol?'* I typed it over and over again. It seemed whoever controlled my hand previously was back; at least I presumed it was them. I then hit 'send' or rather I was made to hit 'send'. I thought that would be the end of it but it wasn't. I was directed to the Internet search bar and my hand typed in *Occult Symbols*. I tensed. Wasn't Occult a bad word, something to do with the devil?

Various pages came up and my hand clicked on the first one – a Symbol Dictionary – there were so many symbols, including a reverse cross, like the ones in the graveyard, its long stem pointing upwards. A symbol for Baphomet, I read, although who or what he was, I had no idea. The star I'd seen too, it was known as a pentagram. There was one on its own and one in a circle. I clicked on the pentagram in the circle and read the following description:

The pentagram is a five pointed star commonly associated with Wicca, Ritual magick, Masonry and Satanism.

Satanism – Satan – that was definitely another name for the devil! And the word 'magick' spelt the wrong way but for a reason perhaps, because it was exactly that – the wrong type of magic? But the pentagram I was looking at wasn't quite right; the one I'd seen was the other way round – reversed. My hand travelled upwards again and typed in *reversed pentagram*. I clicked on another page to read:

… it represents Satan or the world of matter ruling over the Divine, or Darkness over Light.

That was the sentence that jumped out at me, that I was *meant* to see, that I remember so clearly. The reversed pentagram was a symbol used to encourage evil and it was carved into the very fabric of Blakemort, the grounds too – the house itself encircled, nature in league with whatever forces presided, encouraging the weeds and bushes to grow that way, to enclose us. Beads of moisture raced down my forehead. I had to go and tell Mum. Show her what I'd found – the *evidence*.

Snatching my hand back, I stood up, determined to do just that, and then heard a ping as an email landed in the reply box. After a brief pause, I sat down again. Was it? Could it be? Carol was answering at last? I swallowed hard, began to read.

'*Who is this? Why do you keep typing the same thing over and over again? Surely you must realise, Carol passed away years ago.*'

Chapter Twenty-Five

"MUM! Mum! Come and see, you have to come and see!"

I was yelling for all I was worth, tripping over my shoe-laces, as I ran across the hallway. From the kitchen Mum emerged with Aunt Julia, her eyes were red, she'd been crying – again. Why couldn't she just be happy for Dad and Carrie? Why did everything have to be about her? I shook my head, surprised that I'd become so easily distracted. I had to focus – there was something to tell, something important.

"Carol's dead!"

Mum stared at me. "What?"

"Carol's dead. I was sitting at your desk and I thought I'd send her an email. I asked if she was okay and I had a reply, Mum, a reply! She's not okay, she's dead."

Why I was so euphoric I don't know – it was bad news, the worst.

Mum glanced at Aunt Julia and then looked at me. "Let's go and see what you're talking about."

Oh, the ghosts, the clever ghosts! They'd erased the email! Why hadn't I printed it off? I knew how to do that.

I'd seen Mum do it a thousand times.

"Is this your idea of a joke?" Mum said, caught between confusion and anger too.

"No, it's true! I had an email. Honestly. It said she's been dead for years."

Aunt Julia endeavoured to come to my rescue. "Perhaps she erased the email, Hel, by accident, I mean."

Mum ignored her. "I don't know what you're talking about, she can't be dead. She can't. If she is who the heck am I paying rent to?"

Aunt Julia had been inspecting the computer too. She'd gone onto the Internet page I'd been reading. "What's this?" she asked, baffled. "Why are you looking at stuff like this, Hel?"

Mum looked to what she was pointing at. "Me? I wasn't…" Her face clouded. "Is this you, Corinna?"

"I… Yes. I've seen that symbol before, I wanted to know what it meant."

"I don't think you have, why would you have done? It's nasty, plain nasty. There's no way you've seen it before."

She was getting angrier, her cheeks flushing.

"You need to find out what happened to Carol," I said, standing my ground.

"Carol's fine, she's busy that's all. She's certainly not dead. What a thing to even suggest. I'm disappointed in you, Corinna, very disappointed."

Aunt Julia interrupted. "I've seen that sign too… I was going to tell you."

Mum's confusion increased. "What are you talking about?"

"That sign, the pentagram with the circle around it, I've seen it here, in the graveyard."

"Graveyard? What graveyard?"

"It's also in the attic," I blurted out. "Carved into the window frames."

Mum threw her hands in the air. "What's wrong with you both? You're both spouting such nonsense."

"I don't know about the attic, Hel," Aunt Julia's voice was only slightly hesitant, "but there's a graveyard in the grounds, closer to the woods than the house but… even so. There are crosses in there, strange crosses."

"They're inverted," I said. They both looked astonished I'd come out with such a word but then Aunt Julia nodded.

"Yes, Corinna's right, they're inverted, and there are names carved onto them, unusual names, as well as those symbols."

"You knew about this?" There was shock on Mum's face.

"As I said, not about the attic, I had no idea."

"I can show you where in the attic," I piped up, but Mum was still looking at Aunt Julia.

"You knew about the graveyard, about the fact that there's a bloody graveyard on our grounds?"

Aunt Julia's face was as red as the top she was wearing. "Yes."

"When did you find out?"

"Erm… quite a while ago."

"When?"

"A couple of years."

"You've known for a couple of years and yet you've said nothing?"

"No."

"Why not?"

Another look passed between Aunt Julia and me – my co-conspirator. "I had my reasons, but I think it's time to tell you now."

It was, and time for me to tell what I knew too.

* * *

Mum and Aunt Julia went into the attic. Half of me wanted them to, the other half was scared they'd never emerge, but they did, with Mum looking completely shell-shocked, what she'd discovered eclipsing for the moment what she'd found out about Dad and Carrie. I hadn't told her everything I'd experienced here, I stuck to cold, hard facts. One of them being what was in Ethan's wardrobe. That was their next port of call. Ethan was stunned when they burst in, as he'd been playing one of his games, totally immersed, and it took him a few seconds to register what was happening.

Mum went straight to his wardrobe, opened it, and gasped in horror.

"What the fuck…?"

"Oh, God!" Aunt Julia couldn't believe it either.

Mum might have been cross with Aunt Julia for hitting Ethan that day in the graveyard but she looked as if she was the one who could slaughter him now.

"What's wrong with you, Ethan?" she screamed. "What the hell is wrong with you?"

To be fair, Ethan didn't look as if he knew what was wrong with him either – he stared at the contents of his wardrobe, just as stunned.

"Get out," Mum said. "Get downstairs, out of this

room. I'm calling your father."

She followed him, practically on his heels. Phoning Dad, he didn't answer the phone. "Typical!" she said. "He's probably too busy with that tart of his."

"Mum," I reminded. "She's his wife."

"Who cares? Who the bloody hell cares?"

We were all in the drawing room, Mum and Aunt Julia on one faded sofa, Ethan and me occupying the other. The Christmas tree purchased only a week before and fed plenty of water, looked as if it wouldn't last another day. As for the mould, in some places the walls appeared to be an inch thick with it.

"We have to get out," Aunt Julia was muttering, wringing her hands together. I'd focused mainly on Mum up until then but I realised she was just as agitated.

"We have to find out what happened to Carol first," Mum countered. "That's imperative."

"Is there anyone else who knew her – that you know too, I mean? Maybe you can get in touch with them."

Mum shook her head. "She's an old friend from college. I've lost touch with a lot of people from those days."

"Does she have a sister or a brother?"

"A sister yes, Rose, Rose Mathieson. That was her married name if I remember correctly. She's a few years older than Carol. I could try and contact her, look her up in the phone directory, try all the bloody Rose Mathieson's until I get the right one."

"Or we could email again," I suggested, fearing her plan may take a lifetime. "I'm telling you I got a reply."

"But who was it that replied if not Carol?"

Aunt Julia looked at Mum. "I suppose there's only one way to find out."

Mum considered her words. "Okay. Let's do it."

We all trooped through to the morning room, ill-named because night had fallen, had really taken hold. En route, I thought I heard a tinkling of piano music. It was such a solemn tune, familiar too, the hymn Mum tended to favour: *Silent night, Holy night, All is calm, All is bright.* They knew how to mock, those spirits.

Mum sat at her computer and emailed the same address as before, I read as her fingers flew over the keyboard.

I am truly sorry to hear Carol has passed. Could you tell me the circumstances surrounding her death please and when it happened? I'm an old friend of hers and I rent the house she owns – Blakemort. I've been renting it since December 1999 and if she's dead, I'd like to know who I'm paying rent to. I'm very confused. I've emailed this address several times but never received a reply until this evening.

Regards,

Helena Greer

Mum sent the email and we waited with baited breath, even Ethan, who was clearly as bewildered as the rest of us.

"She won't reply," Mum said, chewing at her nails. Anger flashed through me. Why'd she have to be so defeatist?

We waited and we waited, I was beginning to give up hope too and then a reply pinged back.

Dear Helena,

My name is Dianne and I was Carol's former partner. She died shortly after leaving the house. It was suicide. She committed suicide. As for owning Blakemort, she didn't. I don't know where you got that idea. She rented it as you apparently do. You say you've emailed this address several times before but I've never received any correspondence from you until this evening. Perhaps they went straight into the spam folder, I'll

have to run a check on that. If you'd like to discuss this matter
further, I've included my telephone number in the subject line
of this email.

Thank you for getting in touch,
Dianne Parker

Reading the email a second time, Mum grabbed the
phone and started dialling.

* * *

Back in the drawing room, Mum was pacing up and down.

"Dianne doesn't know who we're paying rent to, she's
got no idea at all."

"How'd you pay it?" Aunt Julia asked, biting at her nails
too.

"Just before she left we arranged that I'd send a cheque
every couple of months to a PO Box address Carol sup-
plied me with. And yes, before you ask, the cheques have
been cashed, every single one of them. It's quite a relaxed
arrangement, I suppose. But that's Carol all over. She's
very relaxed."

"Doesn't sound it to me, not if she took her own life."

"No, there is that."

"Do you know why she did it, did Dianne say?"

Mum shook her head. "She was stunned when the news
came through. They'd split up by that time you see, run
into problems. Theirs was a bit of a rocky relationship apparently. Poor Dianne, I think she feels guilty about what
happened, responsible in a way."

Aunt Julia murmured as if in agreement. "How long did
Carol live here?"

"Not even a year, although she gave me the distinct

impression she'd been here a lot longer than that." She shook her head. "But then, as you know, she also gave me the impression she owned it. I didn't think to delve deeper, to ask too many questions, why would I? She was my friend, I trusted her." Sighing deeply, as though exasperated, it was a moment before she continued. "As I now know, before she moved in she was living with Dianne. When things started to go wrong, Carol wanted her own space. This place came up, it belonged to a friend of a friend, and the rent was low, *irresistibly* low." Mum paled further when she said that, at the parallel of it. "Carol thought it was ideal. With plenty of room to stack her canvasses, she could really spread herself out." Again she was quiet. "I can't believe she's dead, Ju. We used to have such a laugh, Carol and me, in our art school days. She was so talented, she specialised in fine art, you know. Portraits mainly. Dianne hardly ever visited Carol at Blakemort. She didn't like it. She found it… *oppressive*. But Carol seemed settled, until she decided completely out of the blue to up sticks and leave, that is."

"How did she…?" Aunt Julia's voice trailed off.

"It wasn't here," Mum rushed the words out, keen to dispel that notion. "She didn't kill herself here. She told Dianne she was going to live and work abroad, just like she told me, that she wanted to do a fair bit of travelling in-between, see and paint the world, get her head straight, her priorities right, that kind of thing, perhaps even settle per-manently overseas. But she never left the country. She caught a train to London, checked into a hotel, one of those big, anonymous ones, stayed there for quite a while actually, a few weeks, and then…" Mum closed her eyes briefly, "hung herself."

Aunt Julia's expression was as pained as Mum's. "Did you say she specialised in portraits?"

"Yes, why?"

"When we went into the attic, I noticed some canvasses stacked up against the wall. An old sheet was thrown over them but it had slipped off, they were easy enough to spot. Whilst you were looking out of the window at the graveyard I went over to look at them, they were portraits too. I didn't like them."

"Why not?" Mum asked.

"Because the subjects all had their eyes closed as if... as if they were dead."

Like the photos then – the ones I'd seen in the attic and those they'd subsequently seen in Ethan's wardrobe.

"What... who are these people?" Mum's voice was a whisper.

"God alone knows," Aunt Julia answered.

I pressed my lips together. It was either God or the antithesis of God.

"There were quite a few paintings," Aunt Julia elaborated. "Old people, children as well, some of them were modern, others historical, dressed in... you know, strange clothes, Victorian, Edwardian. I'm no expert, but I think some clothing dated back even further than that. And all of them had that one thing in common."

Mum stared at Aunt Julia for a few seconds and then repeated her sister's words of earlier. "We have to get out."

Although despair was apparent in her voice, her words were like music to my ears. She tried calling Dad again but got no reply.

"Let's just take the car and go," Aunt Julia suggested when Mum replaced the receiver.

"But what about all our stuff?"

"Your stuff?"

"All our belongings, I can't just leave everything."

Aunt Julia seemed as small as Mum suddenly, no longer statuesque. "I… I don't know, Hel."

Mum shook her head, came to a decision. "I think we're panicking. We do need to leave but perhaps not tonight. Let's… let's just hang on 'til tomorrow. It's really icy and… well, country roads can be dangerous when they're icy. Paul's intending to take the kids out in the morning, so let him do that whilst we pack the essentials. It's much more sensible to leave in daylight. We'll be calmer too, able to think more clearly. It's important to stay rational." Focusing on Aunt Julia, she asked, "I know your place is small, but can we go to yours? It'll just be for a few nights, until we find out what's going on here." Aunt Julia said, "Of course." and Mum sighed in relief.

"We can all go to my room tonight, bunk down tog—"

"Not your room, Mum," I interrupted. "Can't we light the fire and stay here?"

Mum glanced at the ceiling, no doubt thinking about the symbols engraved in the window frames directly above her bedroom and didn't insist otherwise.

Chapter Twenty-Six

ON Christmas Eve there was more terrible news. We learnt that Dad and Carrie had been in a car crash. He wasn't badly hurt, thank God, but she'd received quite a jolt, and there were fears for the baby. We wouldn't be seeing him as planned because he was remaining in hospital by her side. Carrie was distraught, Mum told us, and understandably so, as was Dad.

"I couldn't tell him about Carol," she continued to explain, the rest of us huddled on sofas, shell-shocked too, "or about the house. How could I? He's got enough to deal with. We have to take care of ourselves."

We started packing, just a small suitcase each, Mum helping Ethan or rather just grabbing clothes from his floor and stuffing them in. What presents we had were put into one of those big blue laundry bags. Mum said we could take them too. As for me, I was quite capable of packing my own suitcase and Aunt Julia had barely unpacked. Alone in my room, the whispering started.

You can't leave. You can't.

"Yes I can, I bloody can!"

I'd never sworn before, not really, but I thought I'd give it a go.

There was laughter, the kind I never wanted to hear again. My resolve hardened. Once I'd left and got out of there, I wouldn't go back, I'd refuse. Mum could send in the removal men to get the rest of our stuff surely? We didn't *have* to go back.

I turned to get more clothes and tripped over a pile of books on the floor, books that hadn't been there before. I fell to my knees, landing heavily. Raising my head, I looked around me. Who'd done that?

"You can't stop me," I repeated. And that's when I saw it, even though to this day I try and tell myself otherwise, that it's just not possible – that my eyes were playing tricks on me, fear causing my imagination to go into overdrive. The walls surrounding me were breathing – that's right, *breathing* – in and out, slowly so slowly as if all four had a heartbeat. I gasped and staggered to my feet, continued to pack, but not so carefully this time. Like Mum I just threw things in.

We met on the landing, all four of us, and eyed each other.

"Ready?" Mum asked.

We nodded.

She took the lead. "Be careful coming down the stairs, hold on tight to the bannister."

None of us needed telling.

Walking across the hallway, I could sense so many pairs of eyes on me. *We're leaving.* I fired the thought like an arrow. *And there's nothing you can do about it!*

Fear gave way to elation; Mum and Aunt Julia were on my side at last and Ethan too, in his own way. He was scurrying just as fast as the rest of us.

I half expected the front door to resist, but it didn't, it yielded easily enough – something else that ignited hope.

The car! There it was, our means of escape. We chucked our bags into the boot and bundled into its worn interior. Mum inserted the key and turned the ignition. It started first time and I exhaled in relief, not aware until then how hard I'd been holding my breath.

We're on our way! We're finally on our way.

And I wasn't going to look back, not even a glance.

Moving forwards it became obvious that something was wrong. The car was dragging, making a strange noise. Mum stopped the car and I tensed. We all did.

She got out and went to inspect.

"What is it?" called Aunt Julia.

Mum had bent down but then she straightened up, fury and confusion on her face.

"It's the tyres," she replied, "there's no air in them, they're flat, every single one!"

* * *

I was glad to see Mum still determined. She stomped back into the house, muttering something about a taxi, Aunt Julia following her, Ethan and me following them.

"I've got a card for a local taxi firm somewhere, I'll try and find it," Mum said when we were in her office.

"And I'll phone the train station," Aunt Julia offered. "As it's Christmas Eve, trains will be a bit on the sparse side."

We stood by as they carried out their respective tasks, both of us nearly jumping a foot in the air at the sound of a loud bang – the front door slamming.

Mum was shaken too. "Did you leave the door open?" she asked us.

Ethan held his hand up. "Yeah, I… I think so."

"So why's it banged shut? There's no wind."

Aunt Julia gasped. "Has someone come in, do you think? The same person who sabotaged the tyres!"

Mum glanced at us; clearly worried we'd be frightened by her words. "We don't know the tyres were sabotaged. It could just be… coincidence."

It was obvious Aunt Julia didn't believe that for a minute.

"I'll go and check," Mum appeased, leaving the morning room and walking into the hallway shouting 'Hello'. There was no reply. Not one that she could hear anyway.

I've told you, you can never leave.

"Mum," I called, galvanized into action by the whisper in my ear, "we need to phone the taxi! Right now." We couldn't delay. We *shouldn't.*

Mum returned. "Yes, yes, I know that." She started searching her desk. "Where's that card, where is it?"

"Was there anyone there?" Aunt Julia asked, still fretting about an assailant.

"Of course not," was Mum's terse reply.

Aunt Julia started ringing the station to check the train times, looked at the phone in confusion, and dialled again. "I think your phone's up the creek, Hel. I guess we'll just have to take pot luck."

Mum only briefly looked up from the drawers she was rifling through.

"I'll check the Internet for train times instead," Aunt Julia decided.

"Yeah, we can look up a taxi firm online too, order one that way."

Aunt Julia started frowning again.

"What's wrong?" Mum asked her.

"The page won't load."

Straightening up, I think Mum wanted to scream. "What the bloody hell is wrong with everything today? Nothing's working!"

The phone started ringing.

"I thought you said—"

Aunt Julia shrugged. "I don't know, Hel… it was making a strange crackling sound when I tried it."

Mum answered it and immediately her face was one of concern. "Oh, no," she was saying. "I'm sorry, so sorry. Truly, I… I can't believe it."

A few minutes passed whilst Mum continued talking, she'd turned her back on us, her voice so low it was barely audible. Putting the phone down, she looked at each one of us. "That was Dad. Carrie lost the baby."

Her announcement was as stark as the news.

"Oh, no," Aunt Julia responded. I was too shocked to say anything, so was Ethan.

After a few moments of silence, Aunt Julia took the phone from Mum. "I'll call the station again, check those train times."

Once more the phone was dead.

"Damn it! I don't understand." Her nostrils flaring in anger, Aunt Julia looked at Mum. "You know what, let's just bloody walk shall we? I don't care how far it is!"

Still reeling from Dad's news, Mum sank into her office chair. "Poor Paul, poor Carrie, I feel so bad."

"Well, it is sad, but—"

"No, Ju, I mean it, I feel awful."

Aunt Julia didn't ask it, I did. "Why, Mum?"

I don't know if Mum even realised it was me who'd spoken; she was staring into the distance, a tear trailing down her cheek. "Because I wished for it to happen. I sat in that kitchen, distraught, and I wanted them to be as distraught as me. I *hated* the fact that they were happy." She burst into heart-rending sobs. "What a terrible person I am, what a terrible, terrible person! It's my fault. Everything's my fault."

Aunt Julia rushed to console her. "It wasn't your fault, how could it be?"

Mum continued crying and I felt like joining in – somehow I knew all hope of leaving Blakemort that day was lost. Mum had retreated into herself; so far even her sister couldn't reach her. She pushed Aunt Julia away slightly and stood up.

"I… I just need to lie down. You don't mind do you? I'm sorry…" Her voice trailed away as she left the room.

Aunt Julia turned to me, defeated. "We'd better get the bags in from the car."

* * *

I forced myself to go and see Mum later that day. Standing in the doorway, I looked at her, my shrunken mum, lying in that bed, her eyes fixated on the ceiling, she was humming, incessantly humming.

"Mum," I called but she didn't respond. "Mum," I said again, much louder.

Finally she noticed me. "Go downstairs, sweetie. Go and

see Aunt Julia. We'll leave soon, I promise. But not yet, I can't go anywhere just yet. Run along."

I wanted to hug her, to tell her not to worry about anything, that we'd look after her, Ethan, me and Aunt Julia too, help her to move on like Dad had moved on. But I wasn't brave enough to go further into the room. I wish I had been. I wonder sometimes if a hug there and then might have changed everything.

I went downstairs. Aunt Julia and Ethan were sitting in front of the fire playing a card game. Despite his teenage years, Ethan looked like a little boy again, lost. We all were, perfect fodder for that house in so many ways.

All too soon, afternoon gave way to evening. It was getting later and later, and, despite ourselves, we were growing heavy-lidded. The house around us was quiet. Everything was quiet. *Silent night.* I started biting my nails, something I never did. It felt like we were in the eye of the storm, waiting for something to happen.

Which of course we were.

Aunt Julia yawned widely and then suggested we go upstairs too, that if Mum still wanted to be alone, the rest of us could bed down in my room together.

"We'll be just across the landing from your Mum, close enough, you know... if we're needed."

I nodded and Ethan shrugged. Seeing that she forced a smile, rose and stretched again – making a bit of a show of it. Just as quickly she seemed to double over.

"Ow!" she yelled, her hand reaching behind her. "My leg!"

"Your leg?" I jumped up too.

"The fire! My leg is on fire!"

How? She was close to the fire, but not that close. Had

it sparked and we'd not seen it?

Without questioning further, I rushed over, Ethan did too, me at least expecting to see all sorts of horrors, but there was no evidence whatsoever of scorch marks on the trousers she wore, despite her insisting otherwise, her face a mask of bewildered pain. Helping her to the sofa, she continued to complain of burning, tears in her eyes as gingerly she rolled up her trouser leg. Again there was nothing, although an acrid smell filled the air, reminding me of meat left too long on the barbeque.

I looked around, at the four walls that enclosed us, desperation rising, but who was there to help? No one living, no one dead either. The house had seen to that.

"Aunt Julia, did you ever see Carol? Do you know what she looked liked?"

"Carol? Why are asking me now?" Her breath was coming in short, sharp pants.

"I just… want to know."

"I saw a picture of them together once. She's got short hair, shaggy, pale skin, freckles, pretty in a plain sort of way." Again she gasped, "My leg bloody hurts!"

Short hair, shaggy – the woman standing behind Mum at the window, screaming. Was that Carol? The woman we thought we were renting off, the dead lady, the one who'd committed suicide. I gulped.

"We need to get out." How many times did it have to be said?

I looked at Ethan and he looked at me. He knew it was crucial too. But what could we do? Children are so helpless – at least we were. There was a single scream.

Forgetting her own pain, Aunt Julia sat bolt upright. "Helena," she whispered, and then to me, "Help me up, for God's sake, help me up!"

Quickly I obeyed, so did Ethan.

"We've got to go upstairs," she continued.

Standing at the bottom of the stairwell, we looked upwards. It was dark. Why had Mum turned off the lights? I went to the light switch, flicked it, but nothing happened.

"I think the lights have blown again," I said. "We've got a torch."

"Where is it?" Aunt Julia asked.

It was Ethan who answered. "It's in the kitchen."

"Run and fetch it," she instructed but he didn't move an inch.

I volunteered instead.

As I ran, I refused to look towards the music room, which was also in darkness. Again, there was the sound of a piano playing, mixed in with laughter, not just from the spiteful boy, but so many spiteful others. *Fuck you,* I thought. Like 'bloody', the word sat well with me.

The torch was kept in the utility cupboard. I went straight to it, pulled it open, and searched around. The light was on in the kitchen but it had sunk very low. I needed that torch! Where was it? Behind the bottles of bleach, perhaps? There were so many of them, as if Mum had been stockpiling. Using them to clean the mould, the yellowed kitchen surfaces, and the general layer of grime, invisible to the eye mostly, but there, always there and easily sensed, even by the non-psychic. I knocked several bottles over, they made a loud thud as they fell to the floor but finally my hand closed around the cold metal of the torch. In my hands now, I switched it on, turned and the light bounced off the window, but more than that, a shape at the window – that of a man, peering in and glaring at me, blaming me, as he'd blamed Ethan – but what for? How were we to blame for any of this?

A scream lodged in my throat as I continued to stare, as others joined him, so many others.

You're bastards, all of you!

And you! The words flew back at me. *You're Corinna Bastard.*

I shook my head, blinked my eyes. Argued no more. Instead I got out of there, fled to the hallway, to the foot of the staircase.

"Oh, there you are!" There was so much relief in Aunt Julia's voice when I returned, as if she couldn't believe I *had* returned. "Come on, help me upstairs."

She was limping, heavily. She placed one arm around me, and the other around Ethan, the light bouncing erratically off the walls.

"We're coming," she called ahead. "Helena, don't worry, we're coming."

Upstairs, the torch was barely sufficient, and the smell that hit us was the same as that which had been in Ethan's room, only intensified.

The smell of death.

Yes, I'd grasped that; I didn't need one of the unseen to tell me. And then the words hit home. Whose death were they talking about?

From downstairs something burst into life – a chorus of voices singing.

"What the hell is that?" Aunt Julia screeched.

"It's the TV," I quickly replied.

She turned towards me. "Did you leave it on?"

"No."

"Ethan?"

"I never touched it!"

It was a Christmas song, not a hymn, a pop song, Live Aid: *Do they know it's Christmas?* Just as quickly it died down, the TV switching itself off.

Aunt Julia was shaking. I could feel how violently her body trembled. "Let's focus on your mum," she said. "Helena, Helena, we're here."

We approached the bedroom and the door was shut. Earlier it had been open.

Aunt Julia released us and fell against it, resting her head briefly. She seemed exhausted, no life in her at all. "Darling, are you asleep?" she called. "Helena?" There was no reply. She turned to us. "We have to go in."

I took a step back not forwards. "I can't," I breathed. "I just can't."

"Don't be stupid," she said and I bristled. She'd never called me that before. "Give me the torch."

"Yeah, go on, stop mucking about." There was spite in Ethan's voice too.

I handed over the torch but reluctantly. *Let them go in*, I thought. *Let whatever's in there consume them.* That will show which one of us is stupid.

Don't.

The word flew at me.

Stay calm.

My hands either side of my head, I wanted to scream. What were these voices in my head? Who did they belong to?

Carol?

My own thought was met with no reply. Instead there was silence again as Aunt Julia and Ethan moved into the dark chasm of the room.

"Helena," Aunt Julia called.

"Mum," said Ethan.

The two of them lowered their voices to whispers.

"Where is she?"

"I don't know."

"She can't have gone far."

As Aunt Julia had said, she couldn't have gone far, she was in no fit state. I turned to the left, walked towards the staircase that hid itself away, stood at the bottom of it, and stared upwards again. I could hear something – a faint humming, drifting towards me, echoing in my ears. How I wish she'd stop humming that damned hymn! That hateful hymn! I didn't want to hear it. As much as I used to love Christmas, I hated it now and everything to do with it – people pretending to be happy when they weren't. Mum pretending to laugh and smile when she'd split with Dad, telling us we'd be okay, that we were still a family, a happy family.

She's a liar!

It wasn't my thought but I couldn't disagree. That's exactly what she was. I started climbing, my tread sure, my eyesight adjusting. Whereas before I'd needed the light, now I knew every tread, every square inch; I could have navigated them blindfolded.

The attic door was ajar, always ajar – that strange mix of 'come in' and 'go away' – and I pushed it further open. The light was working; it was on, but more sickly than ever, as diseased as the house, as the ground it stood on. *Death. Always death.* We'd been surrounded by so much of it for so long.

I could hear Mum but not see her, not yet. What I could see were shadows, more than ever before, gathering again for another performance, eager to enjoy the show. There were flies too, hordes of them, not in the air, but crawling over surfaces, their movements not fluid but strangely jagged as though they were part of an old black and white film, the kind that flickers constantly. In the rafters, something fluttered, not a fly, much bigger than that. I steeled myself, inhaled. Let it swoop at me. Let it dare!

"Stop that noise, Mum," I said, my voice impressive, bold.

The humming continued.

"Stop it," I repeated.

When still she refused, I crossed to the box that Ethan had previously opened and reached into it. Immediately my hand closed around the smooth glass of a paperweight, one that Ethan hadn't stolen for his morbid collection.

Accompanying the humming was whispering, soft at first but becoming frenzied.

Do it, do it, do it! Kill her, kill her, kill her! Do it, or we'll kill you!

And then another whisper, more timid: *Don't give in.*

Yet more: *You can't leave. You can never leave.*

The soft voice again: *Try. You have to try.*

I closed my eyes, becoming even more confused. *Try what?*

To kill her.

It was those words that were the clearest.

There she was! I could see her at last. Sitting in the middle of the room, dead centre, with all those strange, spider-infested clothes scattered around her and swaying back and forth, her eyes closed and humming – my mother, my beautiful but weak and lying mother.

It's my fault, she'd said. She'd actually admitted it. *Everything's my fault.*

Something fluttered above her head now but just as quickly it disappeared. On her hair a fly landed, seemed to settle.

I clutched the glass weight tighter and continued forwards, started to hum too. *Silent Night, Holy Night.* No, Mum, no. There was nothing holy about this night.

There was a tugging at my hand but easily I shrugged it off.

Don't, don't, don't.

Ignored too the accompanying pleading.

Even when I stood before her, Mum didn't open her eyes, didn't bother to acknowledge me. Typical of her, she never acknowledged anything.

It's your fault, all this torment. You're to blame.

I lifted my hand, higher, higher still and then, as the whispering turned to laughter, to cheers, to a resounding applause, I brought it crashing down.

Chapter Twenty-Seven

ALL hell broke loose. There were footsteps behind me, screams from both Aunt Julia and Ethan, wild fluttering above, then more screams, but not from the living. Some frantic, others whooping with joy. Amidst all this, Mum never stirred. As for me, I was screaming too; such a strange sound, distant, disconnected, but me nonetheless, my mouth wide open. The object was still in my hands and there was red, so much of it – blood on the floor and blood soaking my mother's hair as her body crumpled, not matching the shade, but turning it darker, so much darker, blacker than black. This was no vision, not like the one I'd had in the drawing room. This was real.

Desperate to regain some kind of control, I threw the glass weight as far from me as possible; heard the thud as it landed in some far corner. I threw myself too, across Mum's body, yelling out for her, praying fervently that she'd be all right.

"What have you done? What the hell have you done?" As much as she was able to, given her perceived injury and all the junk that was in the way, Aunt Julia rushed towards us.

Ethan stood perfectly still. "It's the house," he kept repeating. "It's the house."

Mum stirred. One hand reached upwards and came away smeared. She looked into Aunt Julia's eyes not mine. "Get me out," she managed. "Get us all out."

Thank God Mum wasn't like Aunt Julia, that she was slighter. Between us we managed to hoist her up, Aunt Julia still wincing with every step she took, crying out on occasion. She turned her head to look at me... no, not look... she glared.

"Lead the way," she instructed.

Don't hate her back, don't hate her back, don't hate her back. The words were spinning in my head. *Don't give it anymore to feed on.* And I had, I'd given it plenty. Mum and Ethan too, they'd given it apathy – just as nourishing. But here's the thing – the thing that only now I'm starting to admit. That moment when I held the paperweight up high, my mind had been clear, not encroached on at all. When I brought it down with all my might, not once, not twice, but several times, I'd been elated, the happiest I'd ever felt – powerful, in control for once, and hungry for more. I'd been evil, I'd tasted it, and it was delicious, like the best treat in the world, better than chocolate ice cream, than birthday cake, so much more satisfying. Even the coldness within me had warmed; I was on fire, *glowing*. The boy, that spiteful boy, and me, we were the best of friends after all. And *that* was the worst thing that happened that Christmas. I'd succumbed, become a part of the house – *Corinna Bastard*. There was no one to blame, no unseen entity, no assailant, no possession of any sorts, not this time. It was me, all me. When was I lost? The minute I'd run through the music room door with its blackened surround? I don't think so. But something had set me on my way. And in that room with the eaves windows, I'd almost reached the point of no return.

Ethan broke my reverie, he pushed past me and took the lead, but surprisingly he reached backwards to grab my bloodied hand, to pull me forwards. I think it's the first proper contact we'd had in years, besides a push and a shove, that is. Perhaps he was worried I'd change my mind, run further back into the attic to hide alongside the others. Afraid of the repercussions I would face from the living. I was tempted; believe me, so very tempted.

Again, somewhere in the house a door banged. I was terrified the attic door would shut too and close us in. Those within would fall upon us like ravenous beasts, desperate to gorge themselves on our flesh, to drink from our veins, but that didn't happen. We shambled through it, all four of us, the walking wounded, Ethan flicking on the torch again to light the way. Having been such a commotion, there was again no sound at all; everything was still, so still. I couldn't decide which was worse. We had to go single file down the stairs. Mum only just managing to stay on her feet, colliding with the wall every so often, Aunt Julia ever vigilant, turning round to steady her. On the landing we bunched together again. There'd be plenty of questions fired my way soon but now was not the time.

"Come on," Aunt Julia instructed. "We have to keep moving."

There was another bang and then another.

"Who's here?" Mum's voice was still slurred, as if she was drunk. "Who could it be?"

"No one, Mum," I said, trying to offer what comfort I could. She ignored me. "Mum," I said again, more piteously this time. I had to have one word from her, just one, to tell me it was all right; that she didn't hate me, that she loved me still.

How can she love you now!

"Stop it!" I yelled. "Stop it!"

Before anyone could react to my outburst, light flooded the landing, the bedrooms too, the radio in Mum's bedroom and the TV from the drawing room both started blaring. There was silence no more. The sound was deafening.

"The electrics," Aunt Julia had to shout to be heard. "It's just the electrics, they're as dodgy as the heating. Follow me."

Again we hurried forwards, as much as we could, taking into account the state Mum was in, but then, halfway down the stairs, she stopped.

"Who's that?" she said, her eyes narrowed as though she was trying to focus. "Carol, is that you?"

I could see nothing. "Mum," I urged.

"Carol, it is you! We heard you were dead, that you'd committed suicide. What nonsense! You're here, you're alive!"

"Hel, there's no one there." Aunt Julia tried to reason with her too.

Mum held her hands out. "There is, Ju, can't you see her?"

"Hel—"

"Wait! She's speaking, she's saying something."

I strained to listen too.

I am dead… I'm here. I tried to warn…

Warn? That word struck me.

"It was you, wasn't it?" I shouted. "That wrote those

words, that guided my hand?"

Aunt Julia looked at me as if I was mad.

"There's no-one there," reiterated Aunt Julia, her voice a hiss.

"Hang on," Mum said, "just hang on."

"It's that blow to the head, that's what this is." Aunt Julia was still searching for logic, but I noticed Ethan was listening, intrigued too.

"She's telling me she's sorry," Mum continued. I was amazed she could hear so much better than me. "She wanted to get away, escape, she was desperate. She sacrificed us, offered us up as a replacement, but the guilt was too much. What she'd done, the selfishness of her actions, it overwhelmed her. She's sorry. Over and over again she's saying she's sorry, that she's here, she's still here. That it's hell."

I tugged at Mum's sleeve. "Ask her who the house belongs to?" Maybe that was the key I was looking for, the knowledge that would release us; the mystery owner.

Mum faltered and silently I urged her to hurry. After a moment she spoke again.

"It doesn't belong to the living, that's all she'll say. It's nobody living."

Aunt Julia had had enough. "We're getting away from here. The next house isn't far. What do you think, a mile or two? We have to reach it. Come on."

Mum turned to her, her eyes wide, and full of terror. "Ju, she said the house won't let us go, it'll trap us."

"Rubbish! A house can't trap you."

But it could, in many ways.

Starting to move again, my foot slipped and Ethan reached out to grab me.

"Careful," his voice a loud whisper. "You know you have to be careful."

Downstairs, other noises filled the air, ones that only I could hear. Party noises, people talking, laughing and clinking glasses. Piano music too, definitely piano music, the keys being pounded, not a hymn this time, instead it was an erratic, savage cacophony. We were hurrying towards the door but I couldn't ignore what was happening in the music room. There was definitely a party going on, but not one you'd ever want an invite to. So many filled the room, figures that were becoming clearer, more defined. All wore gowns, like the ones in the attic, some with their hoods up, others wearing masks instead, hideous masks, a few with long beaks, made of something white, could it be bone? It reminded me of bone.

The sight stopped me in my tracks.

"Come on, for God's sake come on," Aunt Julia instructed, but I couldn't move. The shadows, the shapes multiplied, filling the kitchen too no doubt, as well as the other rooms, and in-between them were more shapes – people without cloaks and masks. Naked, the only thing that covered their bodies were sores – black and foul looking, beginning to burst, oozing long thin strands of white. Could it be maggots? Bile rushed upwards but I gulped it back. Such wretched beings, their hands were either side of their faces, as Carol's had been, and they were screaming.

One broke away from the rest – the spiteful boy – no longer a shadow, an outline, or a mere sensation; he was as solid as you or I – as vital. I was surprised at how sweet his face was – his dark eyes framed by long lashes, dimples in both cheeks and creamy white skin without so much as a blemish. I'd never imagined him that way. Never. His smile too… it was beguiling.

It's Christmas Eve; do you want to join the party?

I refused to be taken in by him.

Go away.

Come on, it's fun. We're friends, the best of friends.

I'll never be your friend.

Why's that? Because you hate me?

I hesitated.

Go on. Say it. Say that you hate me.

Again I refused.

Hate is welcome here, as welcome as you are.

I'm leaving. I'm going.

The boy simply shrugged.

Go on then. But you'll return. Making a wide arc with his hand, he grandly gestured to those behind him. *You have to. You're one of us.*

I stepped back, took another and another, crashing into Ethan again.

"Careful!"

I turned and looked at him with tears in my eyes. Incredibly, he softened.

"It's all right, we're going. You'll be all right." At last he was acting the part of the protective big brother. He wasn't calling me stupid. None of this was stupid. It wasn't imagination either. I'd seen. I'd actually seen. And I didn't want to see anymore.

Aunt Julia opened the front door as figures spilled into the hall – the house was bulging with them – and their laughter… oh, their laughter. It would sound forever in my head.

They were at our backs, driving us forward, not concerned at all by our departure. And that was what was so frightening, much more than if they'd blocked our path. Their confidence echoed that of the boy's: *you'll return, you have to.*

Outside the cold air hit us. The trees that surrounded us, the bushes – *in a circle, you're in our circle* – swaying, despite the stillness of the night. And in amongst the trees were more hooded figures, swaying too, and chanting, endlessly chanting.

Legion. Legion. Legion.

"I feel sick." It was Mum. She came to a sudden standstill and heaved violently, the contents of her stomach spilling everywhere. At the same time her legs buckled.

"We have to get you to hospital," Aunt Julia was muttering, her voice shaking as much as she was, her eyes wild. "The car, if only we could use the car."

"Walk," Mum croaked. "Just help me to walk."

Behind us the door shut, groaning as it always did. Unlike last time, I looked back, my gaze irresistibly drawn. The dead filled each and every window, the lights a dull flicker in some rooms but fully ablaze in others, as if flames were devouring them. And Carol, poor apologetic Carol, who'd sacrificed us to save herself, she was no longer screaming but dangling from the ceiling of the upstairs spare room, her legs jerking violently and those around her ecstatic to see it. I didn't need to be in the room to hear the snap as her neck broke, to see the terror, the despair on her face, the sheer hopelessness, or hear the words that were meant solely for me.

This could be you.
This could be you.
This will be you.
It will be.

Unable to look anymore, I followed the others, onto the road that led into Whitesmith, the village proper. The time was one minute past midnight on Christmas Day and white flakes began swirling in the air before us. It was snowing at last, that yearned-for snow, but there was no joy in it. It was just another mockery.

Epilogue

MUM was okay – there was no lasting damage. Knocking on the door of the first house we came to in Whitesmith, the resident was shocked but kind, quickly dressing and taking us via her car into Eastbourne, to the accident and emergency department, her windscreen wipers frantic as the snow became heavier. At the hospital, the usual questions were asked and Mum said it had been an intruder who'd attacked her, who, when rumbled by us, had escaped. So fluently she lied and I was grateful for it, for her protection. Aunt Julia wanted to interrogate me later, in a bid to understand why I'd done what I did, but Mum was stern with her and told her to leave it, just like she'd done once before. She said that she'd deal with me. But she never did. Deal with me, I mean. She never even told Dad.

The story about the intruder served us well, Mum saying that was the reason she couldn't bear to set foot in the house again, and nobody sought to question it. The removal men were sent in to retrieve our items and they were put in storage, whilst we spent the remainder of the festive holidays between Dad's house and Aunt Julia's. During that time I kept catching my aunt eyeing me suspiciously, fearful I was going to attack her next. The bond between us broken, we were yet another casualty of Blakemort, our relationship strained to this day. That stuff we had in storage? Most of it was sent to the tip. We moved into our new house in Lewes in mid-January, a humble two up, two down, but none of us minded. How can you mind normality?

We got on with our lives and Mum's work gradually began to pick up. She even started dating again, but so far she hasn't settled with anyone permanently. 'I like my freedom,' she once told me. I liked mine too, what I have of it.

When enough time had passed, two years, maybe three, I summoned up the courage to ask her. "Mum, what are we going to do about... you know... everything that happened?"

"We bury it, that's what we do, sweetie, and we carry on, we smile, we laugh, and we counteract it. One day it will go away. If we don't talk about it, it will just go away."

We counteract it. It was sensible advice. But at night, when I lie awake, listening to the sound of traffic in the distance, questions go round and round in my head; primarily to whom did the house belong? Not Carol, but someone else – someone not living – Legion perhaps, a collective. But what kind of collective, a satanic coven or a cult? As an adult I know that Legion has connotations with the demonic. When a person suffers possession it is often Legion who speaks through them, a multitude, a mass, demon upon demon – could it be that the same applies to Blakemort? That it was built to house Legion? Blood the cement holding it together. And the spiteful boy, who was he? A leader? How could such evil be wrapped in such beauty?

Ethan never mentioned the house again either, nor his macabre collection. He developed a healthy interest in girls instead. Between them and exams his attention was focused.

I studied hard at school but I also read about my psychic ability – it wasn't diminishing but it certainly wasn't developing either. It seemed to be stuck at some sort of stalemate. After our time at Blakemort, I still sensed things but nothing as malevolent, nowhere near. Thank God. And then I left school, started working, and met a new set of friends – one in particular, with a more defined ability than mine. A friend who 'saw' as a matter of routine, who insisted I had nothing to be embarrassed about; someone who heard every word the spirits uttered, who offered me an opportunity to use my gift for the greater good. The thought really appealed to me – helping those that are grounded. There are just so many in need…

I started working for Ruby, met Theo and Ness too, and became part of the Psychic Surveys team. I even met my boyfriend, Presley, through Ruby's boyfriend, Cash; they're brothers you see, ordinary people, not psychic at all. Or at least I don't think they are. There's a school of thought that says everybody has a psychic ability – Theo's school of thought to be precise. She says it's in each and every one of us but most shut it down, are taught to do so as children. Any lingering insights they have earning them the title of 'stupid', or 'weird', just plain weird. How many times was I called stupid as a kid? As you know, plenty. You shut down or you shut up. It seems most people cannot contemplate a spiritual world existing alongside the material one, not unless it's within the restraints of religion. But it's there all right and at times the veil is perilously thin. I suppose that explains why Mum saw Carol, and why she tolerates what I do now, although if I start to tell her about a case she'll often change the subject. Thinking about it, she changes the subject every time. She just smiles at me. Always she smiles. As I do. Like mother, like daughter.

I've mentioned before that Ruby, Ness, and Theo don't know about Blakemort, or that I've seen and heard too in the past. I haven't been brave enough to explain. Is it still standing? That house marked by death. None of my family have been back; haven't been anywhere near it. When we go out, we head the other way. And only briefly have I searched for it on the Internet – there was nothing of course, no mention at all, not then and not now, as if the house doesn't exist. But it does exist, and I live in fear of Ruby saying, "Hey, Corinna, I've had a call, there's a couple renting a house nearby. They're complaining of the usual, you know, cranky heating, whispering, and footsteps. Do you fancy coming along with me to investigate? It's close by, in the village of Whitesmith. It's got a strange name, it's called Blakemort."

What will I reply? "It's not in Whitesmith, Ruby. It's a lost house in a lost village, and home to the lost. I know because I used to live there, it was once my home too."

That phone call's coming.

I know it is.

The End…

Also by the author

If you enjoyed Blakemort and want to read more paranormal fiction from Shani Struthers, check out her bestselling Psychic Surveys series, published by Crooked Cat Publishing. There are three books in the main series so far: The Haunting of Highdown Hall, Rise to Me and 44 Gilmore Street with the fourth, Old Cross Cottage (working title) coming in 2017. There's also a prequel to the series: Eve: A Christmas Ghost Story or if you prefer romance with a hint of the supernatural, check out the ghostly Jessamine. This Haunted World Book One: The Venetian is also available, mixing fact with fiction, it's set between Venice, 'the world's most haunted city' and Poveglia in the Venetian Lagoon, 'the world's most haunted island'. They're all available from Amazon in e-book format and paperback.

This Haunted World Book One:

The Venetian

Welcome to the asylum

2015

Their troubled past behind them, married couple, Rob and Louise, visit Venice for the first time together, looking forward to a relaxing weekend. Not just a romantic destination, it's also the 'most haunted city in the world' and soon, Louise finds herself the focus of an entity she can't quite get to grips with – a 'veiled lady' who stalks her.

1938

After marrying young Venetian doctor, Enrico Sanuto, Charlotte moves from England to Venice, full of hope for the future. Home though is not in the city; it's on Poveglia, in the Venetian lagoon, where she is set to work in an asylum, tending to those that society shuns. As the true horror of her surroundings reveals itself, hope turns to dust.

From the labyrinthine alleys of Venice to the twisting, turning corridors of Poveglia, their fates intertwine. Vengeance only waits for so long…

Psychic Surveys Prequel:
Eve: A Christmas Ghost Story

What do you do when a whole town is haunted?

In 1899, in the North Yorkshire market town of Thorpe Morton, a tragedy occurred; 59 people died at the market hall whilst celebrating Christmas Eve, many of them children. One hundred years on and the spirits of the deceased are restless still, 'haunting' the community, refusing to let them forget.

In 1999, psychic investigators Theo Lawson and Ness Patterson are called in to help, sensing immediately on arrival how weighed down the town is. Quickly they discover there's no safe haven. The past taints everything.

Hurtling towards the anniversary as well as a new millennium, their aim is to move the spirits on, to cleanse the atmosphere so everyone – the living and the dead – can start again. But the spirits prove resistant and soon Theo and Ness are caught up in battle, fighting against something that knows their deepest fears and can twist them in the most dangerous of ways.

They'll need all their courage to succeed and the help of a little girl too – a spirit who didn't die at the hall, who shouldn't even be there…

Psychic Surveys Book One:
The Haunting of Highdown Hall

"Good morning, Psychic Surveys. How can I help?"

The latest in a long line of psychically-gifted females, Ruby Davis can see through the veil that separates this world and the next, helping grounded souls to move towards the light - or 'home' as Ruby calls it. Not just a job for Ruby, it's a crusade and one she wants to bring to the High Street. Psychic Surveys is born.

Based in Lewes, East Sussex, Ruby and her team of free-lance psychics have been kept busy of late. Specialising in domestic cases, their solid reputation is spreading - it's not just the dead that can rest in peace but the living too. All is threatened when Ruby receives a call from the irate new owner of Highdown Hall. Film star Cynthia Hart is still in residence, despite having died in 1958.

Winter deepens and so does the mystery surrounding Cynthia. She insists the devil is blocking her path to the light long after Psychic Surveys have 'disproved' it. Investigating her apparently unblemished background, Ruby is pulled further and further into Cynthia's world and the darkness that now inhabits it.

For the first time in her career, Ruby's deepest beliefs are challenged. Does evil truly exist? And if so, is it the most relentless force of all?

Psychic Surveys Book Two:
Rise to Me

"This isn't a ghost we're dealing with. If only it were that simple…"

Eighteen years ago, when psychic Ruby Davis was a child, her mother – also a psychic – suffered a nervous breakdown. Ruby was never told why. "It won't help you to know," the only answer ever given. Fast forward to the present and Ruby is earning a living from her gift, running a high street consultancy – Psychic Surveys – specialising in domestic spiritual clearance.

Boasting a strong track record, business is booming. Dealing with spirits has become routine but there is more to the paranormal than even Ruby can imagine. Someone – something – stalks her, terrifying but also strangely familiar. Hiding in the shadows, it is fast becoming bolder and the only way to fight it is for the past to be revealed – no matter what the danger.

When you can see the light, you can see the darkness too.

And sometimes the darkness can see you.

Psychic Surveys Book Three: 44 Gilmore Street

"We all have to face our demons at some point."

Psychic Surveys – specialists in domestic spiritual clearance – have never been busier. Although exhausted, Ruby is pleased. Her track record as well as her down-to-earth, no-nonsense approach inspires faith in the haunted, who willingly call on her high street consultancy when the supernatural takes hold.

But that's all about to change.

Two cases prove trying: 44 Gilmore Street, home to a particularly violent spirit, and the reincarnation case of Elisha Grey. When Gilmore Street attracts press attention, matters quickly deteriorate. Dubbed the 'New Enfield', the 'Ghost of Gilmore Street' inflames public imagination, but as Ruby and the team fail repeatedly to evict the entity, faith in them wavers.

Dealing with negative press, the strangeness surrounding Elisha, and a spirit that's becoming increasingly territorial, Ruby's at breaking point. So much is pushing her towards the abyss, not least her own past. It seems some demons just won't let go…

Jessa*mine*

"The dead of night, Jess, I wish they'd leave me alone."

Jessamin Wade's husband is dead - a death she feels wholly responsible for. As a way of coping with her grief, she keeps him 'alive' in her imagination - talking to him everyday, laughing with him, remembering the good times they had together. She thinks she will 'hear' him better if she goes somewhere quieter, away from the hustle and bustle of her hometown, Brighton. Her destination is Glenelk in the Highlands of Scotland, a region her grandfather hailed from and the subject of a much-loved painting from her childhood.

Arriving in the village late at night, it is a bleak and forbidding place. However, the house she is renting - Skye Croft - is warm and welcoming. Quickly she meets the locals. Her landlord, Fionnlagh Maccaillin, is an ex-army man with obvious and not so obvious injuries. Maggie, who runs the village shop, is also an enigma, startling her with her strange 'insights'. But it is Stan she instantly connects with. Maccaillin's grandfather and a frail, old man, he is grief-stricken from the recent loss of his beloved Beth.

All four are caught in the past. All four are unable to let go. Their lives entwining in mysterious ways, can they help each other to move on or will they always belong to the ghosts that haunt them?

A note from the author

Keep in touch via my website - www.shanistruthers.com - where you can subscribe to my occasional newsletter and keep up-to-date with book releases, competitions and special offers. I'm also active on Facebook and Twitter, it'd be great to hear from you!

16298133R00136

Printed in Poland
by Amazon Fulfillment
Poland Sp. z o.o., Wrocław